*Darkness Falls:*

# UNRELENTING

# ADVERSITY

*BOOK 2*

MARTIN W. FRANCIS

ISBN-13: 978-1539034261
ISBN-10: 1539034267

First Edition, 2015
Copyright © 2015 Dark Storm Press
All rights reserved.
Dark Storm Press
2515 62nd St
Lubbock, TX 79413

https://www.facebook.com/DarkStormPress
https://twitter.com/MartinWFrancis
https://www.facebook.com/MartinWFrancis

Books by Martin W. Francis:

Darkness Falls Book 1: Rise of the Fallen
Darkness Falls Book 2: Unrelenting Adversity
Darkness Falls Book 3: Through the Eyes of the Phoenix
The Fallen: Complete 'Darkness Falls' Trilogy
Darkest of Storms Book 1
Live for Today: Short Story Collection
Forsaken Wastes

Soon to be Released:

# BLOODY

# EVENTIDE

## (EMBER: BOOK 1)

## A NEW 'DARKNESS FALLS' ZOMBIE NOVELETTE

This is for my dad who probably won't notice the dedication until someone tells him. Thanks for teaching me how to fix a car, the difference between right and wrong, how to be strong, a leader, to always follow my heart and my own path in all things, for keeping me safe with a roof over my head, for raising me with old fashioned morals, for your wisdom and advice, for the big things and the small. I know I don't say it often enough, but I love you dad! Thanks for always being there when I needed you.

# Table of Contents

## Introduction

Handfuls of survivors amongst billions worldwide infected have become the norm. Those of us that make our way through the daily hell do whatever is necessary to see another tomorrow. I am one of those few survivors among the living still wading through the abyss. Truth is that even those of us among the living have lost some of our humanity. I'm no stranger to death or killing, but in a world where it has become an almost daily thing it wears on your mind and soul. My name is Jessie Sparks, previously known as Colonel Sparks of the 4th Marine Expeditionary Brigade. My closest companions or sparse family that survived prior to the epidemic called me Jess for short. Strangers simply knew me as the tall, attractive, black-haired, green-eyed, female with the tanned complexion. I had been out of the US on a mission when the epidemic first began. As my team were abroad we watched the news of the massive explosion in New Mexico. Right after it occurred the government barricaded several cities. We paced as we saw the civil unrest unfold. The military back home were sent to restore order in all the major cities. There were several small altercations which led to inevitable deaths of civilians. Among those that died were elderly and children. The everyday citizens of the nation rose up overpowering the military. The government itself soon fell with the leaders and politicians fleeing to foreign countries. We saw a massive blizzard overtake the states spreading the epidemic they called Living Death faster than any epidemic ever seen before. Pneumonia Mortughetlicatis was the medical term for Living Death. The symptoms were similar to pneumonia only nothing seemed to cure the ailments that persisted. Those that were infected became deceased within a matter of days. Once they died, they came back as something no longer human. They became known as the *Fallen* (the name deriving from an evil that had fell upon them taking their humanity). We saw the first media coverage of the undead creatures referred to as the *Fallen* attack a couple in a park. These *Fallen* had a pale blueish glow in their eyes. They attacked with a strength that was incomprehensible. They were capable of tearing limbs from their victims, crushing bones, and ripping the flesh open to feed their blood lust.

We were warned not to return. We were told to stay put awaiting further orders by some General we had never even heard of. Continuously watching all these horrible things transpire we made a decision to return home regardless of orders. Many of the men under my command were seriously worried about their families or loved ones.

On arriving at Altus Air Force Base in Oklahoma my team was overrun by *Fallen* that had once been men and women of the military. I lost everyone that returned with me having to put down the last one the following day back in the states. During an altercation with a Fallen he was bitten which is another way the virus is transmitted. I made my way towards Colorado which is the only place I knew as home. I didn't get very far because the Hummer I borrowed from the base broke down. In Guymon I was traveling on foot when I befriended three brothers; Dan, Kurt, and Sam. The three of them were heavily built, strong muscled men, with similar appearances other than Dan being a little shorter than the others. I stuck with them while they searched for their family. One of the family member they were searching for was their sister Amy. I was immediately attracted to her even before we met in person from an old photograph I stumbled upon in their family home. Yes, she was a gorgeous young white female with short blonde hair (same color as her brothers), blue eyes, a nice smile, and had curves that were unbelievable. Her swim-suit model appearance was only half of what really drew me to her though. I have always been a good read of people. It was important in my line of work to notice every detail that made up a person to identify my enemies especially if they were a terrorist cleverly hiding among civilians. I could tell from the picture that she was a strong-willed woman, worked out often to keep her figure, a tiny bit of a tomboy, very spoiled, was friendly to whomever she met, knew how to communicate, had no problem being honest or open unless it negatively affected someone she cared for, and had a little bit of a kinky nympho side that she kept in reserve only for those she fell deeply in love with.  Finding a letter she left behind, we safely rescued her from a campsite. Unfortunately their father had died sacrificing himself to save Amy. From the first day we met, Amy showed that she was attracted to me. We began building something that quickly developed into a relationship from that point on. From Colorado we traveled to Ruidoso, New Mexico to meet with Ryan Pendleton. The brothers had met Ryan (who prefers to be called Rye) previously in Texas, but it was the first time that Amy or I had met him. He had dark brown hair, blue eyes, and was athletically in shape. He had an almost olive complexion which I later found out was due to his Irish, German, and Greek heritage. On first impression I analyzed that he was a competent leader, intelligent, free-spirited, and a kind man

8

that had endured many hard misfortunes recently. One of those misfortunes was recently losing his wife whom had been the one true love of his life up to that point.

For a little over a year our group created a small community that we called home. It may sound complicated to those who thrive on old social norms, but Amy and I both fell in love with Rye over time. He treated us equally in all things including love. The three of us shared a bond greater than I can begin to describe. During that time of building the community we found other survivors that joined us. We also lost lives of people that had become like family to us. There were a dozen of us and a dog named Tempest, the last time I saw them. Tempest was a pure white half Akita, half wolf, female hybrid that saved a few members of our party from a man who cared only for his own self-preservation. We began to accept our lives as they were with what happiness could be found in a world which had been overran with *Fallen*. During that time a minor military presence moved into our backyard metaphorically speaking. While out on reconnaissance, I acquired intelligence that a new danger from my past was now threatening the survival of my group, potentially every other survivor that might be out there. The weapon had a usefulness in that it could eliminate the *Fallen*, but would also decimating what was left of the human race in the process.

I entered the makeshift military facility constructed at the airport wearing my military uniform hoping to find a way of stopping the danger that the weapon proposed. Inside I met General Ortiz who had once been my mentor and commanding officer. He looked like the same old tough leader I recalled only now had a deep scar that ran across his face. I managed to persuade him into placing me in charge of project 'Raven Storm' of which I had once been part of an oversight committee for. It really was not difficult due to the fact incompetent troops were not yet able to acquire the missing prototype necessary to complete the order given by our President residing in another country to use the weapon on the *Fallen*.

I easily found the location of the missing scientist named Anthony Clayton that had led its development many years ago. I knew him as a friend outside of the project, occasionally having dinner with his family. Leading a team to the location of his lab we found the prototype. I sent the team back to headquarters on a helicopter with an injured man except for one man so not to raise suspicion. The two of us were supposed to be returning the large prototype weapon, parts, photographed equations, and blueprints back to the base on a cargo truck that had been loaded prior to the rest of the team lifting off. I left timed explosives at the lab to make sure nothing overlooked or not taken could be used from the site. On the drive back to the base, I sequestered the cargo truck leaving the officer named Arnolds with only a knife to defend himself. I also made sure he had no way of communicating with the military prior to sending him on his way back to the base on foot. I then returned to the cabins where my group had built our community. They had already left Ruidoso which I had recommended as a precaution prior to entering the military facility in case I failed. Rye left a letter behind in our cabin telling me where they were headed since they had not been certain at my departure. I read the letter stuffing it into a small packed bag they had also left behind. Tossing the bag in my S.U.V., I proceeded to set timed explosives on the cargo truck before hightailing it out of the city.

The explosion filled the sky fifteen minutes later as I pulled over at a gas station just outside the city limits. I saw the familiar black helicopter off in the distance just before turning around to walk into a deep dark forest that lay just beyond the grounds of the gas station. I took with me the duffel bag and an assault rifle slung over my shoulder. My success brought about a smile that lasted for hours walking in those dark woods.

## Chapter 1
## Deep Dark Woods

-1-

I find it difficult to believe how peaceful it is in these woods. Without camping grounds or residential living in the area I have yet to come across any *Fallen*. It has been three days since the explosion of the prototype. I stowed away my military uniform for custom stealth black. I ditched most of the extra military gear I had borrowed from the military base in a fox hole except for the basics to make traveling easier. The black military chopper from the makeshift military base has flown overhead a few times. General Ortiz was even thoughtful enough to send a small search party into the woods at one point. He is obviously grasping at straws trying to figure out my location. I'm sure he is not thrilled that I utterly sabotaged his entire mission beyond repair that the once President of the United States (now known as the Allied Nation after the demise of the government) ordered him to undertake. Now that pompous ass, power hungry, bastard sitting in some unknown country would have to find another top secret weapon to kill off the few survivors left while eradicating the *Fallen*.

13

At the first sign of the search party I quickly camouflaged myself in the hollow of an old broken tree. I hid there for nearly an hour before I felt it was safe. I prepared for the worst making sure I left no tracks of any kind for them to follow ever since leaving the black S.U.V. at the gas station. It seemed like a good ten years since I had been in circumstances like these. I had grown accustomed to giving orders, overlooking projects, and slacking off a little for several years. That changed when I had been reassigned to duty for an assassination mission of a terrorist leader with my team abroad. Since then staying in shape to survive the post-apocalyptic world has prepared me to deal with almost anything that comes my way.

I knew I could take out the entire search party one by one if necessary. However, if I did then all attention would be directed on the woods I was currently hiding in. Instead, I played it safe pretending instead to be the mouse chased by the cat. I have no doubt General Ortiz told them to stay in as tight a formation as they could because the mouse was actually a deadly wolf more cunning and dangerous than the lot of them. Regardless, I kept a step ahead of them, up high, or hidden in plain sight. This went on for almost thirty-six hours before they finally gave up. After they left the vicinity I crept to the edge of the forest at nightfall finding they had flattened all the tires on the S.U.V. and any other transportation nearby.

I took out my map and compass plotting a course in the direction of Salt Flat, Texas where the others had headed. It looked like I was going to have to walk for a couple days cutting through the woods. I would have to find transportation shortly after or I would be in for a very long walk. Starving I had a quick meal consisting of a can of warm potato hash while sitting just inside the woods. My night vision is excellent which made the long walk after the meal somewhat easier since I refused to use my flashlight in the off chance they left someone behind. I continued to walk until the sun began shimmering through the trees. Tying a hammock to branches up high in a tree I took a much needed rest.

After I awoke I decided to take inventory of what supplies might be left in my duffel bag. I found there were only two bottles of water and very little food. Apparently whoever had packed my bag had thought I would be traveling in a vehicle making the trip a pretty short one. I was going to have to find more supplies as well as transportation soon after exiting the woods. I also came across a journal that Rye had written in. It was like a biography of his life. He had apparently started writing it back when things started going to hell right after the explosion. It included everything that had happened since I met him ending with them departing Ruidoso. On an impulse I began writing down everything that I could possibly think of for the last several years including stories or details I had been told by other members of the group. I would find a couple hours out of every day from that day forward to write in that silly little journal if for no other reason than to pass our story on to another if something were to happen to us beyond our control. After a few hours I packed everything back up before I started walking again, only at a much faster pace.

The sun set, darkness fell, and I continued to walk. Early in the morning, three by my watch I came to a clearing in the woods. There had been no problems in the woods other than a large bear I had come across. He seemed hungry, but too weak to attempt to take on a puppy much less prey that would give him a challenge. I was amazed simply at seeing him when wild life has become seemingly scarce. My amazement continued when he glanced my way before slowly trotting off in the opposite direction. I have to admit that I did have my assault rifle trained on him at the time just in case. I would have killed him without fear or hesitation. I could have made a nice bear stew perhaps, but the thought did not cross my mind at the time. It came to me later though in the form of cramps from overexertion and hunger pains.

At the clearing I found no sign of any buildings nearby. All I found was a road that appeared to be endless in both directions. Glancing at my map I saw Mescalero was the next closest city to my location. It would take nearly a day to walk the distance. Hopefully I would find transportation on the road before that.

I hoofed it for several hours before noticing the first building on the main road off in the distance. It took another hour before I arrived at a shanty roadside motel called Hellen's Stayover. It was an old two story home converted into a motel. The place consisted of six bedrooms total; one of which the owner likely lived in year round. She was the only *Fallen* I had to deal with after entering through the locked front door. She heard me when I kicked it in to gain entry. She began banging around upstairs followed by the sound of glass breaking. The door of the room where all the noise came from was locked when I inspected it.

I kicked in the bedroom door which she was standing directly behind knocking her to the ground in the process. Pulling my knife from its sheath I quickly put an end to all the noise that it was making. I commenced to searching the entire motel finding a few supplies to add to my own meager ones. In the kitchen hanging on a pegboard near the back door were a set of keys. Looking out a small curtained window on the back door, I saw a station wagon parked in a stony driveway. I decided it was probably best if I stayed the night to get one good night's rest since I really needed it.

-2-

Rye led the small caravan with his RV safely to Salt Flat within a few hours of leaving Ruidoso, New Mexico. During the drive he discussed with his two passengers Amy and Jerod what they thought would the best course of finding new living quarters for the group. Jerod is an elderly black gentleman with white hair retired from the Texas Rangers and an excellent sniper. They both agreed that the best bet was probably to find another secluded neighborhood as in Ruidoso. Shortly after entering the city limits it became apparent that they would have to drive around to familiarize themselves a little with the area. After thirty minutes of driving with occasional stops to deal with *Fallen* or to move cars that blocked the road, Rye pulled over next to a large sign at an intersection. It had an arrow that pointed away from the main road through town. Below the arrow it stated that there was an airport two miles away. He looked over to his passengers to see if they were thinking the same thing he was.

"An airport would have plenty of room for everyone. It could be made highly defensible like the military did with the one back in Ruidoso. If nothing else we could stay there temporarily until we familiarize ourselves with the lay of the land. Or if everyone decides they are comfortable staying that is always an option," Jerod said aloud what Rye was thinking.

Stepping out of the vehicle Rye walked to inform the rest of the caravan the plan. A few minutes later they pulled up to the main entrance of the airport. The main building was much smaller in comparison to the one in Ruidoso. It looked like the last day it had ran business was a slow one likely due to the population becoming overwhelmed with the epidemic. There were about fifteen cars parked in the parking lot out front. Tall ten foot fencing with razor wire surrounded the area where flights landed or departed. There were three entrances consisting of rotating doors. Along the front of the building there were around twenty panels of tinted glass that could only be seen through from the inside. Several of the panels had been shattered in by the one thing that was a major problem. A small private plane had apparently crash landed near the front of the building leaving scraps of metal scattered all over the place. The force of the impact with the ground had been the cause of most of the seven broken panels.

"Well could be worse. At least it's not a large passenger plane and it didn't actually come in contact with the building. It will take some work, but should be feasible," Dan said

"You always were a glass is half full type of person brother. We should take a look inside before we get to optimistic," Kurt replied patting Dan on the back.

Starlette (a.k.a. Star, a nickname that Rye gave her) walked over to Rye asking if they should leave some kind of message somewhere so that I would be able to find them. She is an eighteen year old female that had a twin named Michael which died protecting Amy while out on guard detail. She has a very white complexion, sandy brown hair, and hazel eyes that change from blue to green depending on her mood or the angle she might be standing.

Rye called Amy over to drive Star back to the sign with the arrow to leave a message for me to find them. He pulled out his sidearm disposing of the infected pilot that was pinned under a large chunk of scrap metal. The rest of them made their way inside the airport. Together they secured each area of the facility. Picking off the *Fallen* as they came across them was rather easy in such a wide area because they were easy to spot from a distance. There were fewer than expected possibly due to several escaping through the broken glass panels. There were a total of seven that had to be put down when they had finished. They consisted of a security guard, a co-pilot, an air marshal, a janitor, and a few passengers that never made their flights.

After disposing of the bodies in a hole dug on the far end of the landing bays, the group decided to take a couple trucks to search for the nearest hardware store for supplies to repair and secure the airport. David asked Rye if he could stay behind to wait on Starlette. David has had a crush on her for years, but still not gotten around to telling her even though she obviously has a crush on him as well. When we first met the young teenager barely a year older than the twins with his black hair, brown eyes, and oriental decent; the three of them had been trapped in an electronic store surrounded by *Fallen*. He had been looking after Michael and Starlette to the best of his abilities who also lived in his house at the time. They were all surviving on

their own without any of their parents left alive to help
them.

Rye readily agreed to let him stay behind with Jerod
while the rest of them went to the hardware store. Rye told
him he should use that time to tell Star how he actually felt
about her. David laughed saying he might just do that.
After finding a hardware store the group only ran across a
couple *Fallen*. They returned an hour later with a load of
lumber and other materials. Amy and Starlette had returned
while they were away. Everyone pitched in to help unload
the trailer which they had found hitched to a vehicle at the
hardware store. The owner was unlikely to mind if it was
borrowed. Everyone boarded up the glass panels whether
they were broken or not. Those were further secured by
welding thin metal sheets to the buildings frame that
separated the panels. They place them all the way across
the entire section reinforcing the wood. The broken panels
were insulated from the inside sheet rocking them closed as
a finishing touch. Jerod welded two of the rotating doors so
they were unmovable. Then he welded rods to the frame
and the door spaced only a few inches apart so that if the
glass on the doors were broken it would still be impossible
to enter the building. At the main entrance they placed a
wedge to keep the rotating doors from spinning unless

someone on the inside moved it to let them enter. To secure the glass they used the same metal sheets on the glass sections of the doors that they had used on the glass panels of the building. Before welding them Kurt cut them to fit including a small rectangular section that allowed a person to look outside. By the time everyone finished they were exhausted so an early dinner was prepared before searching for places where each person would be semi comfortable to retire for the night.

The following day the party set to work clearing the small parts of the private plane by hand. Eventually, the group had to use forklifts they found in one of the hanger bays along with other equipment to clean up the larger parts. Rye moved his RV and another one that was found nearby to block the main entrance leaving only a small space to squeeze between them. Sam cut the lock on the only chained opening in the fencing surrounding the landing area. It was barely wide enough once opened to fit the vehicles from the parking lot through. It was quite a bit of work moving the vehicles since the keys that went to them could not be found. A few car alarms went off in the process which had to be disabled by removing the power lines from the batteries. When they were done the project was completed by replacing the broken lock on the fence with a new one. There was now a perfectly clear view in front of the airport. More importantly there were no places for unwanted guests to lurk in the shadows. After a late lunch everyone commenced to putting up wire fencing around the front. It was extended to about fifteen feet including an entry gate with a lock. It took half the following day to completely finish the project. Using an extendable ladder from the facilities management building out near the hangers, Rye made his way up to the roof of the airport's main building. A few in the group carried up materials for those up top who were working on building a small makeshift guard tower made out of wood. Securing a hoist device to the roof they brought up one inch thick; three foot by three foot; plates of steel. They were welded around the frame of the wooden guard tower for maximum protection in the slight chance any living were to show up armed with guns. Once completed anyone with an automatic weapon could technically defend the airport even if they were not the best shot.

The flight tower was converted into a secondary guard post and lookout. Someone that was handy at using a sniper rifle could easily pick off assailants or spot trouble long before it arrived. Although keeping fairly busy for five days straight, everyone was becoming worried that I had still not arrived. Among them, Rye and Amy were going stir crazy fearing the worst. Rye had almost convinced himself into going back alone to search for me. Amy told him to wait a few more days as she was worried that she might end up losing both of us. Jerod is the one that actually talked Rye into waiting just a little longer.

-3-

After a good night's rest I loaded up my things in the station wagon. The forest finally thinned out around the road as I drove. I glanced back in the rear view mirror one last time at the deep dark woods I had recently spent many nights in. A couple hours later I came across the city population sign for Salt Flat. As I continued to drive I was starting to realize that I had no clue where the group were at. I was beginning to think that I might have to drive around for a couple days before I spotted some kind of sign of their presence. I was just considering hunting for a map to figure out where the most secluded neighborhoods were when I came across the airport turn off sign. On the front someone had used a permanent black marker to write the first letter of my name really big. Pulling over to inspect the sign I found that on the backside of the sign was A.P.

Didn't take a genius to figure out the group was at the airport.

I was expecting a large greeting with excited faces, but the small fortress they had built was almost as breathtaking. I knew it must have taken a lot of hard work from a single glance. Amy was the first to rush out to meet me. She nearly knocked me over as she ran to throw her arms around me when I got out of the car. Her embrace was tight as I hugged her back. The others shortly followed which ended up as an awkward group hug. The last to greet me was Rye slightly limping behind the others. I barely managed to escape the group hug to make sure he was alright.

"What happened Rye? How badly are you injured?"

Rye gently put his hands on both sides of my neck while kissing me several times. "I am perfectly fine love. Just sprained an ankle overworking myself. I'll be right as rain in a couple days. We have been so worried! I almost went back to look for you. Another day and I would have gone regardless of who tried to talk me out of it."

"I'm fine, hun. I'll tell you and the others all about it over lunch."

Everyone listened intently as I told them everything that had happened since arriving at the main gates of the airport back in Ruidoso starting with being greeted by men not thrilled to see a stranger approaching the makeshift military base. They must have been lacking in entertainment because they had me repeat the story several times. They hung on every word having a ton of questions each time I told the story. They all filled me in on their own versions of what they had been up to since I saw them last. Later that evening after everyone had wound down from the excitement, I wrote a little in the journal before going for a walk around the airport. I came across April whom looked somewhat distraught.

April is light skinned, late twenties, has wavy red hair and dark green eyes. We met her not long ago while on a trip across country scouting for other survivors to join our community. The other two survivors we found with her that joined our community were Kyle and Thomas. Kyle is a skinny white male, early thirties, with dirty blonde hair and grayish eyes that wears a pair of eyeglasses that should probably be replaced. Thomas is a Hispanic male, early twenties, with brown hair and brown eyes. He doesn't that doesn't talk very much. We found the three of them living on a bus in an RV park near Las Vegas, Nevada. One of their friends had been bitten about to turn into a *Fallen* while they were somehow oblivious to the fact that the infection could be spread that way. Rye dealt with the problem rescuing the group before they all lost their lives.

April waved at me as I walked in her general direction.

"Didn't say it earlier, but glad to have you back Jessie."

"Thanks, it's good to be back with the group. Although, blowing things up is never dull either."

"Funny and gorgeous. I see why Rye and Amy find you so irresistible."

I laughed immediately comprehending that she was not trying to hit on me. "I am guessing that you are being over-zealously sweet because you want something, right?"

"Smart too! Feel like going for a real walk? Perhaps a stroll outside the airport where others might not overhear us talking."

"Sure, I don't mind."

Unlocking the gate out front, we walked a short distance from the airport. April began talking while slightly blushing. Turns out that she was crushing on one of Amy's brothers. She didn't want to specify which one so she asked round about questions. Would have been easier if she just told me from the beginning instead of having to piece together from the questions she asked and watching her reactions to my responses. The conversation was long enough to have walked a pretty good distance from the airport. Coming to the area where the private airport road meets the highway there were several acres of land covered in tall weeds off to the Southeast. We both stopped turning around back in the direction of the airport.

Unbeknownst to us one of the intelligent *Fallen* (a few are capable of detecting dangers like a gun, comprehending certain words, capable of running, and tend to lurk about in the shadows among other things) had been watching us while kneeling down among the weeds out of sight. The moment we turned around it came running in our direction. I barely picked up the sound of its footfall in time to react at all. Reaching for my gun, I realized that I had left it back at the airport where I had taken it apart to clean it. I shoved April who was inches away from being bitten. That was followed by swiftly kicking the *Fallen* in the chest knocking it to the ground. I tried not to focus on the gory sight of loose flesh hanging off of its face as it got back up off the ground. I suddenly remembered my boot knife which I grabbed in a hurry to defend myself. Two more *Fallen* of the slower sort must have overheard the commotion. They came at a hurried pace from an off-site parking facility West of the weeded area called Discount

Parking Depot (that charged less than the airport to leave your car while out of town according to the sign out front). I lunged at the one with the loose flesh hanging from its face. It dodged backing away a few feet. The other two were quickly gaining ground only ten feet away now. I flipped the knife in the air catching it by the blade. In a split second I tossed the knife at the intelligent bastard. The blade struck him piercing the skull. It spun around in circles swatting at the knife for a few seconds before it dropped without moving again. April who had fell down when I pushed her was in shock up until that moment. She suddenly screamed pointing behind me. Without looking I side-stepped making a sweeping arc behind me which turned out badly. From my position all I succeeded in doing was knocking the closest one right on top of me. I quickly braced a hand on its throat keeping pressure so it could not get close enough to bite me. I knew these things were extremely strong so I only had a few seconds to get out of the predicament. I saw a decent rock about the size of my fist on the edge of the road just barely out of reach. Making a rolling motion I ended up on top of the gnashing creature that was just beginning to scratch at my arm grabbing its throat. It left deep cuts with its filthy long jagged fingernails. I reached over with my other hand grabbing the rock before proceeding to smash its brains in. I was in such a rage that I forgot about the other one. It was inches away from my neck breathing the most horrid breathe I ever recall smelling before it registered on my warning radar. I tried to roll to the side which succeeded in keeping my neck from being bitten. However, the damn thing still managed to recover its failed attempt fast enough to rip a large piece of flesh from my shoulder as I rolled. In excruciating pain I tripped over the most recent one I had killed with the rock falling to land near the first one. I grabbed the knife from its skull just as the last *Fallen* came at me for the rest of its meal. I plunged the knife blade into its eye socket at an upward angle twisting for good measure. Not sure how many times I stabbed the thing in its head after killing it, but at some point I blacked out. The rest of the details of what transpired were later filled in by Rye.

Seeing all the *Fallen* dead and me laying there bleeding, April hurriedly got up running back to the airport as fast as her legs would carry her. Rye was the first to hear the jumbled words from April who was now in tears. Catching enough to know that I was injured he took off on foot to find me. The few others headed to the secured fencing where the vehicles were housed. When they arrived a couple minutes after Rye they found him holding me in his arms gently caressing my hair.

She's been bitten Rye! None of us can help her. I'll do what needs to be done if it's too hard for you."

"You're talking like she has already turned Sam. Don't let your sister hear you talk like that. As a matter of fact don't let her see Jessie like this either. Go distract her. Do whatever you can to keep her away. That's what you can do for me."

Sam didn't say another word. He hopped in one of the two trucks they had rushed here in. He took off hoping Amy had not overheard the crying plead from April. He had personally dragged April back here to show them where to find Jessie. It was of course also because he didn't want his sister to find out immediately if it was really bad. Rye picked me up carrying me to the bed of the other truck. Jerod had kept it idling ready to drive back to the airport as fast as possible. April climbed into the front passenger seat. Rye walked up to the driver side window.

"I'll ride in the back with her. Get us to the nearest clinic or hospital you can find."

"Rye…"

"Just do it Jerod."

Rye hopped into the back of the truck. Jerod sped down the road tossing everyone around on occasion. Fifteen minutes later, he pulled over at a small twenty-four hour clinic. Rye grabbed a shotgun from inside the truck using the butt to shatter a window to gain entry. He came back ten minutes later with a bag full of medications and syringes. He ordered Jerod to rush back to the airport. Jerod sped back at a frightening speed pulling into the back gated area which was still wide open. Rye asked April to wait in the truck for a few minutes before coming in worried word might travel to Amy before he could deal with the problem. Jerod followed closing behind Rye opening doors when he came to them. Arriving at the on-site medical facility room, he laid me down on one of the patient beds. He then sent Jerod to find Dan immediately locking the door the moment Jerod left. A knock came at the door a couple minutes later.

"Rye, this is Dan. Let me in."

"Amy?"

"Jerod is keeping her preoccupied for the moment. I gave him a sedative if she goes bat shit crazy once word gets to her."

Rye opened the door letting Dan inside.

"Good god, she looks white as a ghost."

"She lost a lot of blood between being bitten and until the time I got there. I've kept pressure on it as best I could with my shirt and belt. I'm type O negative if she needs blood."

"Rye, you know there is no cure. She probably has a few days at most before she turns if she doesn't pass away before then."

"I grabbed a little of everything I could find at a clinic. Just tell me what each are commonly used for please."

Mostly as an attempt to calm Rye down he started going through the bag of vials and pills listing off their various uses. Rye set certain ones aside until Dan had gone through about half of them.

"Give her something to keep her knocked out for a while, a large pain reliever, the rabies shot, the chemotherapy injection, and the strongest antibiotic there is. Then you can take whatever blood you need after you clean the wound and bandage it up."

"That is a strange variety of medications. I definitely wouldn't advise it. There is no way to know what kind of negative effects it will have on her"

"Negative effect? You mean like turning into a Fallen? Her chances of survival as we currently know it are zero, Dan. I'm not an idiot. Just do it. Radical times call for radical measures. If it doesn't work it won't be because we didn't try something. Please!"

Dan nodded his head before getting to work. He swiftly did as Rye asked. He waited last to give the chemo injection after pouring an entire bottle of alcohol on the wounded area. The needle was inserted directly into the wound. He finished bandaging up my arm before rifling through the medical cabinets. He told Rye to lay on another one of the beds while he set up an IV to transfer blood from Rye over to me.

Right after he finished setting up the transfusion, heavy beating came at the door.

"You let me in there, right now Dan!"

He recognized Amy's voice immediately. He started to walk over to the door as she began screaming obscenities.

"Hey! What the hell was in that…needle?" There was a pause between her last two words. The last word came out almost as a whisper before there was a thud on the ground. Apparently the heavy sedative had done its job. She would be sleeping for a couple hours at least. Dan cracked the door open finding Jerod sitting on the ground with Kurt standing over Amy holding the needle. Kurt had a red mark on his face where he had been slapped.

"She's going to be even more pissed when she wakes up Dan. I don't plan on being anywhere she can find me. We probably should make April's scarce around here too. Amy is likely going to try to kill her." Kurt reached his hand out helping Jerod back to his feet. "Sorry Jerod, forgot what a firecracker she can be when she's angry."

"It's alright. Everyone handles grief and pain in different ways. I understand very well. How is Jessie doing Dan?"

"Well she hasn't turned yet if that's what you're wondering. Rye had me inject her with numerous medications. The combination may kill her off quicker than the bite would have. Will just have to wait and see. Currently giving her a transfusion using Rye's blood since she lost a lot of her own. All we can do now is wait. Speaking of waiting, if one of you wouldn't mind relieving me in a couple hours it would be greatly appreciated. Probably need help getting Rye to his room as well after the transfusion. Get someone to bring some water, maybe a couple of those oranges we picked from that orchard back in Ruidoso a week ago. He will need them."

Kurt bent down picking Amy up. He carried her off over his shoulder. Jerod told Dan that he would come back to relieve him making sure the items he requested were brought as soon as possible. David brought the water and oranges having to be shooed off with his many questions. Dan attempted to strap me down the best he could with a sheet he cut up so that he didn't have to keep an eye on me every second being in fear he might get bitten if I turned.

From the moment I blacked out, I began having a lucid dream of the deep dark forest I had recently been in. I wondered through it with the moonlight briefly shining through the opening of the branches above. In a small clearing, the moon was visible overhead. It was a bright full moon shining down on a very small lake that kept the trees somewhat at bay. I stood there in awe at the beauty of its shimmering reflection on the water. A growl came from behind me. Turning quickly I saw the bear that I remembered seeing in the forest. It raised itself up standing on its hind legs while only about ten feet away from me. As I stood frozen in fear, the bear transformed into something half bear and half *Fallen*. Its eyes glowed blue, there were patches of missing fur, and it was covered in blood. There were several places it had parts of its flesh missing enough that the bones were visible. It dropped back down on all four coming at me fast. I knew there was no time to escape closing my eyes for the inevitable. I could feel it sink its teeth into my shoulder ripping the flesh away.

A moment later I was high in a tree that I had spent one of my nights in attempting to sleep while persistently being uncomfortable. Rustling noises came from the leaves and brush below. Glancing down I saw the forest floor was full of *Fallen* scrambling about. There were hundreds of glowing blue eyes everywhere I looked.

Somewhere in that darkness I felt Rye grip my hand calling out my name. His voice led me to better dreams leaving the forest behind.

-4-

Dan tried to talk Rye into leaving to get some rest when Jerod showed up, but he refused. He told him that he could just as easily rest where he was. Jerod told Dan that it was fine. He promised to keep an eye on Jessie until someone came to relieve him in six to eight hours. Kurt relieved him carrying in a newly fueled oil lantern just as the candles were running low that Kyle had dropped off when it started getting dark.

"What time is it?"

"Thought you would still be sleeping Rye. It's around two in the morning."

"How is Amy holding up?"

"After she woke up from whatever was in that needle she went on a warpath. She found April sitting around in the lobby where she beat the crap out of her pretty badly before several of us could pull her off. April had a black eye, a bloody nose, and a handful of missing hair. Dan had to sedate Amy again because she was so hysterical. He is now keeping April company in one of the RV out front locked tight until we figure out what to do. Between you and me, I think he may have the hots for her. I suppose she's attractive, but definitely not my type. Oh sorry Jerod, go get some rest. Not trying to make you wait around while I talk all night."

Kurt and Rye talked for a while after Jerod left. Rye eventually went back to sleep. Dan came in the room bringing the two of them coffee in the morning. He found that both of them were awake playing cards at a small table across the room. He checked to see if I had a fever while asking if I had stirred at all. They told him that I hadn't.

"She has a rising temperature. Likely the first sign of the epidemic. I suppose it could be from the wound and the body fighting an infection too. I'm trying to stay optimistic at least for you Rye."

"I appreciate that Dan. If you would mind giving her more of the same medications except the rabies would be highly appreciated."

"We need to get some fluids into her as well. Will have to look around and see what I can find."

"After you do that you can return to your other watch duty. Pretty sure I can handle keeping an eye on her for a while since I got some sleep."

"Are you sure?"

"Yeah, I slept a lot longer than I wanted to. I suppose I will go talk to Amy while you figure something out for the fluids. Hopefully I can calm her down a little bit. Perhaps get her to give it a rest with beating everyone up. Then again I might be next on the list for not letting her see Jessie. I just don't want her here if she does turn. Don't want to take the chance something might happen to her as well. Will probably sound selfish and one-sided if I tell her that so better come up with a different way to word it on the way to go see her. Looks like we will have to finish the game tonight or tomorrow Kurt." He stood up stretching. "Be back soon Dan."

Soon turned out to be two hours. The conversation with Amy was emotionally intense whether yelling or crying. It was hard to calm or comfort her. Rye did his best to convince her that April was not at fault. He explained that she had no control over the Fallen any more than the rest of us did. She had just been in the wrong place at the wrong time. Rye explained everything that they were doing to help me regardless of what the obvious outcome would likely be. He didn't want her to get false hope either. He discussed with her how hard it had been to put down someone he had loved. Rye made it clear that he didn't want her to have to go through that. He told her that he would have everyone keep her updated if anything changed. If I did turn then she was welcome to visit with me for as long as she wanted once Rye had done what needed to be done. He left kissing her on the forehead while she started crying for the third time.

## Chapter 2
### Heroes & Villains

-1-

Another day passed as Rye patiently waited holding my hand at the bedside. He talked to me despite the fact that I was unconscious. I awoke in a dark room finding myself secured to a bed with handcuffs and leather belts that made it impossible to move much, if any at all. I felt a mild pain coming from my shoulder which made me tense up griping the hand which held my own.

"Rye? Amy?"

"It's me Jess. Sorry I was starting to doze off. Let me light up the room a little." He let go of my hand moving around in the darkness. Turning on a solar powered lantern he set it near the bed on a nightstand. "Now I can see you. How are you feeling?"

"I feel fine. A little groggy and some pain in my shoulder. How long have I been out?"

"Three days since we found you."

"Seriously? How can that be? Shouldn't I have turned by now? I don't even feel sick. I thought everyone who was infected with the Living Death had symptoms similar to pneumonia."

"Well, you did have a fever but we got that under control. I'm not sure if we accidentally stumbled on a cure with all the meds I had Dan give you or if perhaps you carry an immunity. I honestly can't fathom the odds of either occurring. Regardless you haven't had any symptoms. It is a miracle that I definitely will not question. We should probably wait one more day just to be sure."

"Think you could untie me? At least long enough to go to the restroom. Some food would be nice too, I'm starving. If I start showing signs of the Living Death then you are free to tie me up again. Or if you're just feeling kinky"

"Surprised you have a sense of humor so soon after everything you went through. Seriously though, it's no wonder you're starving. Dan has been giving you liquids intravenously the last couple days. Let's see if we can find you some real food."

Rye untied me from the bed. I was a bit lightheaded needing assistance to make it to the restroom. After having a small meal I felt much better when moving around. I filled him in on the details of what had happened on the walk with April. I had no doubt he would want to verify the story April had relayed to everyone to be true. He told me about Amy taking out her anger on several people; April getting the worst of it. I felt pretty guilty until Rye told me that something good may have come from it though. He said that Dan was spending a lot of time with April. At first to take care of her wounds. Then to keep her safely away from Amy. Rye told me about the emotional discussion he had with Amy to calm her down. However, Dan was still using uncertainty to keep April locked up in an RV where he spent most of his time.

"Those two belong together. We just have to convince Amy to let April date one of her brothers."

"You can be pretty convincing when you want to be," Rye winked making me laugh while I was taking a drink of water. The water went everywhere.

The following day I was still showing no signs of infection. Everyone was in complete bewilderment at seeing me walking about as if nothing had happened. Amy of course broke down in tears of joy while hugging me tightly for I can only assume a good twenty minutes. After a long group discussion with Dan acquiring more of the same medications they had given me became a top priority in case they had actually stumbled across a cure that no one else had been able to figure out.

The next day a large party went out in search of those medications and other supplies. I stayed behind not ready to deal with another encounter right after somehow just surviving one. They came back with much needed rations apparently having only a few encounters with *Fallen*. During the next week a new greenhouse project was started similar to the one we had back in Ruidoso. Everything was pretty quiet at the airport for the next couple months while we began to become comfortable with our surroundings. The men transported a large quantity of furniture into the airport to make accommodations feel less like we were living in a transportation depot. Everyone found their own special living quarters which they redecorated to their own tastes to feel a little more at home. We turned the airport restaurant into a large dining area with an atmosphere more to our liking. It was one of several places for everyone to gather and socialize as a group. Rye requested a trip to a library or a bookstore. Luckily there was a bookstore just a couple blocks down on the highway. Somehow we ended up with our own small library. The security room at the airport became the weapons room for all the spare weapons we had hauled with us from Ruidoso, plus the new ones we had acquired since then during our supply runs. We hit up a water bottling company on the outskirts of town returning with several trucks full of water. It took a while but we eventually came across a fuel tanker truck with much needed gas we would have to use sparingly. Even with additives to extend the fuels life it was starting to weaken having sat unused for such a long period of time. Alternative modes of transportation would likely have to be found by next year that did not require electricity or gas. Kurt and Sam found themselves a couple of motorcycles to save on fuel for the time being.

With the arrival of November the snow began to fall. The details of what had happened to Rye's wife was shared among the group so that the same mistake would not be made. We rarely left the airport except when it was absolutely necessary. One of those occasions was to find a large supply of blankets, dry lumber for a vented indoor fire pit we had set up, and warmer clothing for everyone. There was not one individual that was sad to see the end of the snow or the cold weather that lasted for the next couple of months.

Coming up on the second year since the explosion that changed the world and all of our lives, we tended to the greenhouse so we would have our first crops of fresh food. Finding the nearest water supply to accommodate watering the crops and transporting that water was no small task.

When the rain first fell in April we all noticed the change. The dangerous sweet odor and blueish glow we had become accustomed to were no longer part of the storms. It seems the atmosphere has managed to purify itself of whatever it had absorbed from that explosion, providing it had not mutated into something now undetectable. Rye proceeded to test the theory himself under heavy protest from everyone, myself included. After spending an hour in the rain he did end up catching a cold which lasted for almost a week. The next time it rained everyone was outside in the gated in area where flights used to come and go; playing in the downpour like they were children experiencing it for the first time. It was a short rainfall, but the rainbow that filled the sky afterwards was vividly colorful.

So many factors of peacefulness and stillness around us put us at ease within our secure environment. By June we had a large garden ripe to pick. We ate our first fresh spoils. Nothing seemed to ever have tasted so good. Many spent their time reading, exercising, or making runs to search for supplies further out in groups. During the first week of July, Jared was alone on night security as we had lessened our guard detail down to one person. We had come to the belief that there was no threat while we were safely inside these walls. Just as everyone was settling in for a good night's rest we heard a gunshot. We setup a system a long time ago that if it was *Fallen* we would use a silencer to not draw the attention of others or so that the group would not worry they were in danger. No silencer meant there was a danger or the threat was of the human sort. Fearing the worst everyone sprang into action immediately. Rye rolled off the bed grabbing the hand-held radio while I threw on clothes like it were a military exercise.

"Jerod, what's going on out there?"

A couple more gunshots were fired shortly after followed by what sounded like an all-out war. I missed any response that might have been given by Jerod. Grabbing my assault rifle, I headed to the main entrance while others were still getting dressed or armed. Climbing inside one of the RVs I peered out a curtained window counting four sets of headlights. One of the vehicles had smashed through the fencing before crashing into the other RV. The driver side door stood open with a man lying dead on the ground with a rifle nearby.

Just as I was about to enter the fray of whatever small battle was taking place someone fired a hand-held rocket launcher that created a large explosion from where Jerod was stationed above. I quickly exited the RV while gunfire commenced around me. Crawling under the RV, I took position near the truck that had broken the barricade. I stayed low to the ground hopefully out of sight. Turning on night vision on my rifles scope I quickly found the individual that had used the rocket launcher. With my silencer attached I had time to take him and two others out before they caught on that there was a new assailant somewhere attacking them. The remaining individuals climbed into two of the vehicles trying to escape just as the rest of my group piled out of the airport. Rye got off a good shot hitting one of the drivers as they were speeding away. The driver yanked the wheel when the bullet hit him making the truck flip over on its side. The other truck managed to escape regardless of how many rounds of ammunition my group wasted trying to stop them.

Looking back I saw there was nothing left of the makeshift guard tower once erected on top of the airport roof. I ordered Thomas to find a ladder to see if there was any chance Jerod had somehow survived. He might be up there injured for all we knew. As a group the rest of us went to inspect the truck that was lying on its side a good distance away.

Arriving at the truck we found the driver dead. The front passenger had been thrown through the windshield were he lay dead some twenty feet away. In the backseat cab area there was a woman who was injured, but alive. We pulled her from the wreckage after finding she had a pulse. She remained unconscious as Sam carried her back to the airport. I told David and Kyle to gather up any of their weapons they could find. I picked up the rocket launcher and two remaining rockets myself, just being cautious they were handled properly. The others kept watch while we cleared the area of anything else we could find in the vehicles or on the dead bodies. Each corpse we came across we shot in the head so they would not come back as *Fallen*. Two of them which I had not shot were found already having sniper bullets pierced through their skulls presumably from Jerod. Thomas was just coming down off the roof when we were returning.

"No luck?"

"Sorry Jessie, he didn't make it. Found what was left of him clear across the roof."

"Was his head still attached to his body?"

"Good god, are you serious? It was a smoking charred corpse. Yeah, I guess it was why?"

"Go back up there and make sure he doesn't turn. He deserves to be at rest. We will bring the body down tomorrow after we dig a grave."

Thomas shook his head not thrilled at the idea of having to go back up the ladder, but went none the less. Kurt rushed off ahead of the rest of us. Rye followed walking at a fast pace behind him. Curious what the hurry was Dan and I looked at each other. There was a good possibility that many of the others would love to see the injured woman dead. Dan had made a Hippocratic Oath and knew his brothers all too well. I had an alternative reason for wanting to make sure she survived. She was the only link to the ones that got away or the details of what danger they might pose to us. We nodded heading inside the airport finding neither one of them were anywhere in sight. Amy was across the way from the entrance near the back doors.

"Did you see where Kurt and Rye went off to?"

"They went out to the hanger bay where they do repairs for planes. Sam took the girl out that way a little before they went by. I guess they went to interrogate her or something."

Both of us rushed out the doors past Amy who followed not far behind. It took a couple minutes to make it there on foot being so far out. Would have been a shorter trip if we had thought about the golf carts parked in a nearby storage building. I was not at all surprised to find the woman chained up with her arms raised above her head while hanging a foot off the ground by a hoist with a hook. I was perhaps a little surprised to find the group at each other's throats. Rye had Kurt pinned to the ground with his arm behind his back. That alone made Dan raise his eyebrows seeing how as Kurt was twice Rye's size. David and Kyle were standing in front of Sam trying their best to not let him get by them to help Kurt. He punched Kyle in the gut making him fall down curling up in pain. He then threw David to the side like a rag doll. Starlette stepped in front of him from out of nowhere giving him an 'I dare you' look. Just as he reached out to push her aside, Tempest growled loudly from behind him baring her teeth. He froze slowly turning around. Seeing her he lightly stepped away from Starlette no longer attempting to make an advance towards Rye. He stood there glaring angrily with his fists clenched tightly.

Watching all of this shocked the three of us that had just stumbled upon this whole predicament. Obviously we had missed whatever transpired to lead up to the conflict. Amy walked straight over to Sam slapping him in the face. He didn't seem to even notice as he continued to glare. She slapped him again, this time as hard as she could getting his attention. He commenced to complaining that he needed to help Kurt. She slapped him a third time.

"Shut up! Kurt is perfectly fine. You try to lay a finger on Rye and I will cut it off before I feed it to Tempest."

At hearing her name Tempest sat down on her hindquarters licking her chops. Sam raised a questioning eyebrow, but stayed silent without moving. Dan and I walked over to where Rye was holding Kurt down. I kept an eye on Dan just in case he should become overly protective like Sam.

"Hey guys, what seems to be the problem? I'm surprised to see you're losing brother."

"Just get him off me already."

"Sorry, Kurt you do realize Jessie is standing right here. She would beat us both senseless if I even tried to help you. Besides I know both of you pretty well. Rye wouldn't intentionally put anyone in this position unless he had a damn good reason. So tell me what dumb thing did you do to put yourself in this situation?"

He just laid there not answering Dan's question. I knew exactly how stubborn thick skulled people like Kurt worked.

"Go ahead and let him up Rye. We can all be civilized while having an adult conversation right Kurt?"

"Yes, fine. Whatever."

"Of course if you do anything stupid I will put you on your backside in a split second. Are we clear?"

Kurt simply nodded his head. He knew I had bested him every single time he had tried to take me on during the training exercises I had given them back in Ruidoso. He also knew that I was a person that meant what I said. If I was joking it was always clear. None of the group, even Rye know how truly dangerous I really can be or how many lives I've had to take. It is better that they don't. Rye let go of his arm before standing up. He took a few steps back to slightly distance himself. I noticed he was standing between where he had left Kurt and the female who was being held captive.

Dan put his hand out to help Kurt up after he rolled over. Kurt ignored him upset that Dan hadn't attempted to defend him. He stood up on his own without assistance.

"So?"

"So what?"

"So what happened knucklehead?" Dan was getting clearly frustrated at having the question avoided.

"Nothing. It was just a misunderstanding."

We turned our attention to Rye.

"Rye, hun. Why was Kurt pinned to the ground?"

"Even though we are friends and basically family I had no other choice."

Kurt hung his head down in shame embarrassed after hearing Rye's words. Looking back and forth between the two of them I noticed the very large mechanics wrench nearby on the ground.

"Exactly what was the plan with the wrench Kurt? Were you going to beat to death an unconscious defenseless chained up girl? That is not something I would expect from you. You're better than that. The two of us are also like family. For the first time ever, I am ashamed that you are basically a brother to me."

He looked up with pleading eyes that began to tear up a little.

"I'm sorry. I wasn't thinking clearly. I was in a rage from everything that happened especially that Jerod was killed. When I saw the wrench the only thought that came to mind was to break her legs so she couldn't walk, couldn't escape, and couldn't kill anyone else. I was so angry that I picked it up intending to do what I thought was best for everyone at the time. Thank you for stopping me from making an idiotic mistake I would regret forever Rye."

"Apology accepted. Everyone makes mistakes."

The two of them awkwardly shook hands before Kurt walked off towards the airport alone.

"Well, if I didn't know he already felt tremendously foolish or you hadn't already torn into him good, I would've knocked him upside the head for good measure. Brother or not that is some messed up thinking. Now for the other one. How about you let me handle Sam from here provided Amy hasn't already beat the crap out of him. I swear you women are as tough as nails. Rye here is pretty good at handling himself, but he doesn't stand a chance if he gets on the wrong side of either of you."

"Actually the way I see it, if I ever come across something I can't handle I know they both have my back. I'm lucky because with either of them at my side I know I'm going to win."

"That's a good response Rye," I gently elbowed him in the side while giving him a wink.

We all laughed for a moment before Dan walked over having a couple words with Amy. He then grabbed

Sam by his ear twisting it while pulling his head in a downward motion. Sam was clearly pissed now, but Dan put him in a headlock telling him to try something if he dared. He walked towards the airport pulling Sam with him while he had a quiet conversation that only the two of them could hear. Starlette dusted David off before wrapping his arm around her neck to help him up. He had a slight limp as they head off next. Thomas who had showed up after our conversation with Dan went to check on Kyle who was no longer curled up but was still lying on the ground. Amy came over giving Rye a big hug.

"Sorry my brothers can be complete cavemen sometimes."

"Not all of them. Dan seems to know how to handle a situation properly while thinking clearly. He has an interesting sense of humor too."

"He used to be worse than the other two, but he grew out of it. He still scares the crap out of them though because they know he can be the exact opposite of his seemingly nice natured self. The times he did flip his lid those on the opposite side usually wound up in the hospital. I thought Kurt had grown out of the stupid anger crap too, until I saw him pinned to the ground. I knew he had to of done something completely moronic. What did he do anyway?"

"I'll explain while we walk gorgeous. You coming Rye?"

"No, you two go ahead. I'll be there in a little while. Can you get someone to do something about the opening in the fence out front? We need a replacement for guard duty as well. I doubt they will come back the same night, but we need to stay on our toes until they are dealt with. We can move the vehicles they left behind tomorrow."

"We will make sure everything gets taken care of. You just try to relax. Take time to process all those thoughts spinning around in your head. I think I will work on convincing Amy about that thing we discussed a while back involving setting up two little love birds."

"Seriously? You had to go there and put another thought in my head? It is going to be extremely difficult to think about anything other than you convincing her now. Thanks, Jessie."

"That was the point love. You know where we will be." I winked at him trying to convince him to join us. We both kissed him before walking back to the airport's main building.

As Amy and I walked, I explained why April had asked me to take a walk with her the day I had been bitten. I let her know that after several indirect questions I was convinced that April liked Dan. I then went over the details of how Dan had reacted after she had beaten April up pretty badly. Amy was still upset that I had been bitten in the first place because April had wanted to go for a walk. She was even more pissed that it happened the same day that I had shown up from Ruidoso. She had been so worried something had happened to me. Then when I showed up safe she had been overwhelmed with relief only for that to be ripped away. Logically I should have died turning into a *Fallen*. She asked how I would have felt if things were reversed. I told her I probably would have beat the shit out of April which made her smile. She then relayed that she was also probably a little overprotective about who Dan might date. I told her that April wasn't a bad person. She was also probably just as lonely as Dan. Plus there were not exactly a dozen possible women to choose from as might have been the case prior to the epidemic. I made my case by telling her that if anyone deserved to be happy it was Dan.

"Fine, I might be willing to accept the two of them together. Of course I might need some convincing too."

She winked at me catching on to the innuendo with Rye a few minutes ago.

"Oh, no worries. I plan to convince you over and over until you scream yes at least a few times tonight."

The following day we made plans to set the two of them up since they were both avoiding the fact that they both liked each other. Our plans were forthcoming as we did little things to nudge them into conversations or bringing them together only to leave them alone. During the funeral we had for Jerod a couple days later, Dan held April in his arms while she cried. After that they were practically inseparable.

As for the woman in the hanger, Dan patched her up. She came around the following day, but had as of yet been cooperative in any way. We treated her respectfully despite the circumstances. She was moved to a secure room where she was unbound. She was given food regularly anytime we ate as a group. Although she was free to move about the room there was no way to escape or anything left lying around that she could use as a weapon.

Following the funeral I went by to see if I could convince her to talk. I opened the locked door finding her ready to pounce. Unfortunately for her I was armed pointing a gun in her direction since I sort of expected her to try something sooner than later.

"Have a seat so we can have a friendly chat."

"I would rather stand if you don't mind."

I entered the room closing the door behind me while standing in front of it.

"Fine by me. I'm curious are you military? Your posture seems to suggest that you have had some kind of training."

"I served time in the Army Reserves to help pay for education. Why do you ask?"

"Glad to finally run across someone else that was in the forces. Think we might have a civil conversation?"

She sat down crossing her arms looking at me curiously. "You're the one that took out most of the men the other night I'm guessing. What branch did you serve in?"

"I'm Colonel Sparks of the 4th Marine Expeditionary Brigade among other titles I used to carry. Dealing with terrorist groups, high profile targets, and weapons of mass destruction were a daily routine."

"Figures, guess I'm lucky to still be alive."

"Do you mind if I ask why exactly your group attacked us? The only witness we had from when it began seems to have found himself on the wrong side of a rocket launcher."

"To be honest the group I was with are complete imbeciles. I likely would not be in this predicament otherwise."

"Oh, how so?"

"The group I was with were out scouting the area for supplies when we came across the airport sign. We figured it would be overrun, but we were in a bad way for food which is also why we were scouting at night. We completely ran out over a day ago. The others thought we could handle any number of *Deadheads* with all the ammo they were packing, so they decided to come check out the airport. I protested suggesting we hit up residential areas instead. They were the type to not really register a woman's opinion. The only reason I even traveled with them was because of the security in numbers factor. Anyway, I believe that the individual in the tower fired a warning shot initially. The shot went off right around the time we got close enough to see the airport was obviously occupied by the living. One of the individuals apparently didn't give a rat's ass if your man was shooting at a bird. He drove his truck right at the fence full speed crashing through it while ramming into an RV in the process. He jumped out pointing a rifle up at the tower which got him killed in an instant. Whoever was up there was one hell of a shot with reflexes like a cat. After he dropped to the ground dead the others that were with me went crazy. They hurriedly got out of their vehicles using the trucks as shields. Bullets started flying after that as they commenced to firing at the individual in the tower. Despite all the men trying to kill the person up there, two more of ours went down. I had no clue that we even had a rocket launcher. Regardless, one of the men thought it a bright idea apparently to finish the task with a damned rocket. The rest you know. I never even got out of the vehicle."

"Very intriguing story. Most would likely believe you were attempting to make yourself appear innocent in the attack to hopefully find lenience. Lucky for you, I've had a lot of experience with profiling people and the whole interrogation process many times over during my service. I'm extremely good at reading people through body language, gestures, reactions, and speech patterns among other things. Since you are being so forthcoming let me ask you how many got away in the other truck. Do we need to worry they will be coming back with reinforcements?"

"Normally I'm the type of person that wouldn't give up information easily probably even if threatened to have my teeth or nails extracted. However, I never truly became close to any of that group. I have no allegiance to any of them and to be quite honest I don't even like them. The only person among them I sort of got along with was Kate. Sadly, she is pretty much brain washed into following along with many others. To be clear the reason I am even having this conversation with you right now is because I need to get away from that group. They are going to end up getting everyone killed. Hopefully your group is a better one providing you are interested in new members joining. To answer your questions, two men got away the other night. As for them returning, there is a high chance that they will. The main group usually stays on the road acquiring what they can find while we travel. Overall there are fifteen men and three women at camp plus the two that got away the other night back."

"I appreciate your candor and that you are willingly being forthcoming. I admire the loyalty you convey that you would give to true comrades or loved ones. I would not have held it against you if you were silent because of that loyalty. Luckily for us they were not worthy of being loyal to. Sounds like we are going to have our hands full pretty soon with some unwelcome guests. I can't promise this Kate person you mentioned will not be a casualty if she attacks with them. I can promise that the group I am with are nothing like the ones you have been traveling with. They would treat you with the same respect that they are given. Once you had their trust there is not one of them that would not give their life to protect you. Given a chance we could even be friends."

She looked at me skeptically. I wouldn't simply believe the words of someone I just met, especially after coming from a group that sounded like there was not one decent one amongst the lot. Only time and actions would show her the same truth that I am able to easily acquire from reading people. Trust is something that is earned not given freely.

"I would like that if you're being sincere. I'm Aurora by the way."

"Jessie, but you can call me Jess if you prefer. You hungry Aurora? Let's go grab a bite and introduce you to the others. Just don't make any sudden movements or seem apprehensive at least until I explain the details to everyone. You have to understand we just had a funeral today for the friend we lost."

"What was their name? I'd like to know more about them when there is time if you don't mind."

"His name was Jerod."

I smiled at her seeing that she genuinely was interested. I had a feeling we were going to be very close friends in time. I led her to the restaurant area where I found Rye, Amy, and Kurt having lunch. Rye looked at Aurora starting to stand up, but after a quick glance in my eyes sat back down. I could tell Kurt was not in the least bit thrilled at seeing her moving about freely. However, he did not make a move or say a word.

"It's alright. You know I would not have let her out if I was not a hundred percent certain it was safe and the right thing to do. Amy if you would be a dear and gather the others. We need to have a group discussion."

"Alright love. Be back in a jiffy."

Amy gave me a kiss heading out the open framed entrance to the restaurant. I sat down next to Rye taking his hand. Aurora lifted a questioning eyebrow glancing at Amy as she left and then at Rye. She sat down across the table from me.

"It's complicated hun. There will be plenty of time to explain."

"As long as you're not going to tell me that you are part of some hippy love-for-all cult where everyone sleeps with everyone then I'm good."

Her words made Rye and myself start laughing.
Kurt who had been taking a drink from a warm beer can
nearly choked as it went down the wrong pipe. It came out
his nose and mouth at the same time which made us laugh
even more. We were all laughing when the first of our
group showed up. The others soon followed not far behind.
Our side of the table filled up with many standing directly
behind us wary at the thought of sitting near Aurora. After
they all arrived I stood up moving around the table to sit
right next to her. Rye, Amy, and even Kurt got up moving
around to our side of the table. Kurt scooted his chair
intentionally close to Aurora. When they both looked at
each other there was an obvious attraction between the two
of them in that very moment that I gleamed. Those that had
been standing took the seats we had vacated on the other
side of the table.

I commenced to telling everyone what I had learned
from Aurora pertaining to the details I had been filled in on.
I explained in minimal detail how I was capable of reading
if a person was telling the truth. There seemed to be some
doubt that I could so easily tell if someone was lying from a
few of the looks I got. For the fun of it, I let them test me to
show them exactly how it worked. I explained to them to
that they should tell me a true story, but change a few

things up. They were quite surprised at how well it actually worked. In the end there was no doubt among anyone that everything Aurora had told me was true.

Introductions soon followed amongst the group. Many new questions were then directed towards Aurora. They were all curious about her past, how she survived since the downfall of civilization, and of course details about the other group that would likely soon become a threat.

-2-

Aurora answered the best she could each question that was asked. She even responded to Kurt inquiring if she was seeing anyone. The short description of Aurora is that she is a white female, thirty-one years old, blonde hair with slight strands of faded pink dye, blue eyes, a couple of tattoos (one of which I later saw on her back left shoulder that I recognized as the INSCOM Five-Hundred and Thirteenth Military Intelligence Brigade insignia), five-foot seven, a hundred thirty pounds, very athletically built, and apparently is a Virgo thanks to Kurt's line of questioning.

She served six years in the Army Reserves starting at the age of eighteen. After the Reserves she finished obtaining her bachelor's degree in English. She had ironically published a fiction novel about the living dead titled 'Deadheads,' which was the term she had previously used during our conversation alone. Apparently, she had sold a couple thousand copies while attending small conventions where she signed autographs and talked to fans prior to the epidemic. She did not in the least find it humorous that her fiction had become a reality of sorts.

She described how she used aspects of her military training along with her once imagined details of surviving in an apocalyptic world to her advantage. She filled us in on coming across the group she had hooked up with. Details of everything that she could recall for the last six months (the time she had been traveling with them) were freely given. She explained why she believed they were a threat, specifically the leader they followed.

His name is Stanley Cartwright, more commonly referred to as Preacher. Prior to the epidemic he had been an anti-government fascist protester when he wasn't preaching to a small congregation. As the leader of the group he takes religion and his position to extremes. He believes that only those who follow him are chosen to survive in the new world. Those who do not agree with his views are quick to disappear. The rest of the group are pretty normal for the most part, but they will do anything to survive including stealing from others to take what they need. There are a few with extremely violent tendencies. Stanley has expressed to the majority that they are all forgiven of past or future sins as long as they continue to follow him. That of course has often given the overall wrong message to the group. Some of the violent ones take his word so greatly to heart they show no remorse while they plunder, ransack, rape, or murder. The Preacher shows no empathy for anything the group does despite their transgressions. At the same time, the reason that the less violent majority do not simply throw aside Stanley for new leadership is because he technically protects them from the violent individuals. He has made it clear that the one thing he will not tolerate from anyone (and that is a crime God will make them burn eternally in hell for) is if any of his followers harm others in the group in any manner. Any crime against his followers from within or without is taken seriously always ending in death for the transgressors. He is excellent at putting on a facade or using persuasion with his words or actions. To any person that doesn't know him the Preacher seems like a normal, nice, intelligent, and friendly guy. He only shows his true colors while hidden amongst his flock. Another reason the group as a whole follows him is that he somehow always manages to provide for everyone.

After a short discussion of where the other group were last located it was agreed that their camp was most likely no longer in the same area. We sent out a scouting patrol just to be sure finding the location abandoned a few days prior according to various signs left about the campsite. We then began sending out small parties as an attempt to find their new location.

One of the parties were Kyle, Thomas, and Sam. Around eight that particular evening they should have returned. A little after nine it began to get dark. Worried Rye, Kurt, and Dan went out to the vicinity they were supposed to be scouting. While driving they came across a beat up old car surrounded by five *Fallen* who seemed intent on getting inside. One had just shattered the window on the driver side when they pulled up next to the car. A large pair of bloody hands struggled with the *Fallen* as it stuck its head in the window. Dan was the first to shoot out of the vehicle on seeing a gold class ring with an emerald inset exactly like Sam wore. He yanked the Fallen backwards tossing it to the ground before he proceeded to thrust a knife into its throat until the head was completely severed. He was paying no attention to the other Fallen around him. Luckily for him the others were quickly out of the truck behind him. Kurt disposed of two with a machete he was wielding. Rye took the others out with his pistol.

Dan opened the car door finding Sam covered in blood that was soaked down his shirt. He was holding one of his hands tightly against his chest. Kurt rushed over next realizing it was Sam. All three of them carefully removed him from the car carrying him to the back of the truck. He was as pale as a ghost. Kurt and Rye struggled to remove his hand so that Dan could examine the wound. Someone had pierced one of his lungs likely with a knife from the looks of it. There was nothing Dan could do to save him. Regardless he bandaged the wound after giving him a shot of morphine. Dan took the others aside to explain the situation.

"I don't have the supplies, the knowledge, or the time to help him. If there were a fully staffed emergency room with surgeons he would stand a chance. The only thing I was able to do is make sure he wasn't in pain. He has lost too much blood and isn't going to last for long."

Kurt asked Rye to drive while they rode in the back to say their goodbyes before he passed away. They all agreed that they should continue looking for the others. Rye drove slowly doing his best to avoid potholes in the road.

He only sped up when necessary due to the occasional *Fallen*. Several blocks away Rye pulled over. He got out puking up his meager dinner all over the ground while bracing himself against the truck. Dan and Kurt stood up in the back of the truck to see what all the commotion was about. Two wooden crosses stood in front of a church where a group of *Fallen* were devouring two men that had been nailed to them. The men hung low enough so that they could be eaten alive while their heads were out of reach so that they would turn into *Fallen* themselves. It was Kyle and Thomas with their chests ripped open. Flesh and blood were everywhere. Organs were being fought over by *Fallen*. Bones were exposed giving the appearance of gory broken skeletons with heads stuck on them. While they were staring with disbelief Kyle's eyes opened with a blueish glow.

"Get back in the truck Rye. Don't look in their direction. Just get us the fuck out of here. We have to get back to the airport." Rye stood there hunched over barely hearing the words spoken to him. Dan reached over putting a hand on his shoulder. "The others could be in danger Rye. Get us back for Amy and Jessie's sake. Come on, move your ass."

Hearing the names of the women he cherished above all else broke through to him. The overwhelming sickness subsided instantaneously. He jumped back into the truck.

"Hold on tight to something. Keep Sam secure if you can."

With that Rye gunned the truck. Instead of turning around he went straight for the crosses. He mowed down as many Fallen as he could while plowing right through the crosses crushing them underneath the truck as he continued forward without slowing. It was a good thing that truck was built for strong impacts having a heavy duty grill guard. He turned at the end of the block heading back in the direction of the airport with his foot to the floor on the accelerator. A few blocks away Kurt banged on the back window motioning to pull over.

-3-

I wasn't one to wait around patiently while others were out on a search and rescue mission. Becoming antsy at the airport I went out to canvas the perimeter for any signs of an enemy. Aurora tagged along since she felt cooped up being that she was used to traveling all the time.

There was an ominous feeling in the air. I wasn't the only one who felt it either.

"It feels like there is a large group of Fallen nearby in hiding or something really bad is about to happen. I have that electrified hair standing on ends feeling going on," Aurora said.

"Something is definitely not right. I feel it too. I hope the others get back to the airport soon. Maybe I should radio them."

"They haven't been gone for very long. Give them a little longer. That is unless the feeling gets stronger I suppose. We both have good intuition. Something is out there and an impending threat, but it's something that's on the way, not right on top of us yet."

"Maybe we should do a little recognizance on foot. Would be less noticeable than driving around like an open target. You up to following that intuition to its source?"

"I'm game if you are."

I pulled the Hummer over parking it along the road facing back towards the airport in case we needed to make a hasty retreat. Both of us armed ourselves (fully automatic weapons with silencers) before hoping out of the vehicle. We trotted at a fast pace turning between a couple businesses. Then we entered the alleyway from a back gate heading down it in the opposite direction of the airport. At the end of the block we both stopped. Stealthily checking the street we saw nothing threatening. We crossed the street continuing down the next alley. Aurora who was currently in the lead as I watched our backs came to a halt. She gave me the sign to stop and be silent. Then she gestured to the right silently letting me know there were two assailants. A small stream of smoke rose above the fence line at a distance. Peeking through the cracks in the wood I saw two men smoking on the side of a warehouse. They stood next to a large dump truck. Aurora recognized them as part of the group she had previously been associated with. She signed to let me know they were enemies. We retreated a little out of hearing distance.

"They are planning something. Not sure if they are gathering things for a planned attack or if it is about to go down. Either way that dump truck is part of the plan from the way they were looking it over."

"I agree. We need to take them both out and disable the dump truck so that no one else is capable of using it. First let's check the area to make sure there are not others nearby."

Aurora nodded her head in agreement. We finished walking the alley at which point we quickly crossed the street darting to the opposite side. Completing the other alley adjacent the only threat we found were two Fallen of which we silently disposed of. We made our way full circle back to the fence behind the warehouse. The two men were already in the dump truck just starting it up. Apparently the fuel was old or the truck had mechanical problems seeing how it did not want to turn over. Watching them in the truck's side view mirrors, we snuck through a gap in the fence while they were preoccupied. In seconds we were standing directly behind the back of the dump truck completely out of view. The passenger got out slamming the door back shut. I dropped to the ground getting a perfect view of his legs. I saw him walk to the front of the truck where he lifted the hood obviously from the creaking sound it made. This was the perfect chance since the passenger was out of view from the driver. I shot him in the ankle making him fall to the ground. Before he had a chance to yell in agony I put a bullet in his head. I signed to Aurora that there was only one left. After a couple minutes the driver grew impatient calling out to the other man without getting a reply. He got out of the truck to see what the problem was. The moment I saw his feet touch the ground walking towards the front of the truck I motioned to Aurora. She swept around the side of the truck taking aim.

The driver saw her for a split second in the mirror after closing his door before he was lying in a pool of his own blood. With that done we flattened the tires, took the keys, and cut the brake lines for good measure.

"That leaves eighteen to go. Still have that feeling, but it isn't as insistent as before. There have to be a few more somewhere. Let's get back to the Hummer, Aurora."

We retraced our steps back to our transportation. Hopping inside we back in the direction of the airport. A blocks away I noticed a black van with limousine tint which had not previously been parked where it now currently was sitting. I pulled over letting Aurora know we had another problem. Just as we were thinking of a plan, four men got out heavily armed watching down the main road for something.

"I think they are waiting on the dump truck," Aurora remarked.

One of the men pointed saying something to the others. All of them quickly ran to the opposite side of the van out of view. Moments later I heard someone speeding towards the airport from one of the side roads. Worried it was more enemies, I started up the Hummer shifting it into drive. We slowly crept towards the van.

The speeding vehicle came into view a moment later which I immediately recognized as the truck Rye had left in. For some reason they began to pull over about twenty feet from the van. I figured it was because he realized the van was out of place, but when he got out of the driver side door he headed towards the back of the truck where I noticed Kurt and Dan were sitting. My crawl turned into an all-out full speed frontal assault. I saw the tips of two guns peak out from the front of the van. Rye and the others were completely unaware of the threat. Being caught off guard they lifted their hands in the air momentarily. The brothers suddenly ducked down into the bed of the truck. Rye rolled beyond the tail of the truck drawing a gun while spinning around. I saw Dan popped up with a rifle the same time Rye came slightly around the rear end of the truck with his pistol pointing in the direction of the enemy. Two gunshots went off a split second before I rammed the Hummer into the van at an angle that made it slide sideways and forward. The impact likely killed the men that had been standing in front of it. If not I did not slow until the van toppled over onto its side crushing whatever was left of their party.

Hummer's are usually pretty resilient to damage. I messed this one up pretty bad. Smoke and small flames were immersing from the engine compartment. I was a little shaken up from the airbag that had gone off. I looked over to Aurora finding she had a bloody gash on her forehead. She appeared to be dazed as blood poured down into her eyes obscuring her vision. I shook myself fully aware. Grabbing my knife, I cut her seat belt hurriedly pulling her from the Hummer as far away as I possible could. Arriving to the back of Rye's truck there was an explosion from the Hummer which was now roiling in flames. The explosion knocked us on our backs while I was still pulling her. Looking up I saw Dan ducking down hovering over Rye who sat with his back against the truck. One of the two shots I had heard had been a bullet that hit Rye in the arm going straight through.

Seeing Aurora's head wound, Rye told Dan to stop fussing over him and help her. He turned around seeing that Aurora had a serious injury quickly going to work to help her. Pulling myself off the ground I found Kurt in the back of the truck with tears streaming down his face. In the back of the bed Sam's lifeless corpse was motionless/

"Kurt…Dan, I'm so sorry."

Dan turned looking up at me.

"He just passed a few moments ago."

Hearing Kurt's words I could tell from the look in Dan's eyes that he didn't know yet. He shook his head sadly going back to helping Aurora. Kurt climbed out of the truck. I went to comfort him which made him tear up even more when I gave him a hug. I kept one hand on my side arm and one eye on Sam's corpse. The oddest thing is he never did turn like everyone else that I could recall doing after they died. The thought would puzzle me secretly putting into question the idea of my own possible immunity for a long time.

"Is Aurora going to be alright?"

"Hey there Kurt, I'm doing wonderful," Rye attempted to brighten the mood while injured himself.

"She'll be fine Kurt. Don't mind Rye, I've seen worse mosquito bites than the injury he has," Dan threw out his own humor attempting to downplay everything that had just happened to calm himself.

The others at the airport hearing the explosion shortly came flying down the road in our direction after looking through binoculars to see what had transpired. They were armed in case there was any further unknown dangers. They hurriedly got out to assist in whatever way they could. I stopped Amy from getting to close to the truck. Kurt who had dried up his tears put a hand on my shoulder.

"I got this. You make sure they get Aurora and Rye back to the airport safely."

I nodded walking away to let him tell Amy about their brothers demise. I made sure they were extremely careful loading the injured up. I heard Amy scream before she began to cry. Looking back I saw Kurt comforting her as I had done for him. He let her go so she could come to me. I held her for what felt like forever. Most everyone returned to the airport. I told Kurt and April whom were the only other ones left to take the truck with Sam's body back to the airport.

"Are you sure? It is a couple blocks away. There is no way to know if there are more of them out there."

I'm sure. There are not more of them nearby. Trust me. Check on Rye for us. Tell him we will be there shortly."

"Alright Jessie."

I no longer had that feeling of danger. They drove off in the truck. We eventually started walking back to the airport holding hands. Half a block later a *Fallen* came running our way. Amy was still preoccupied with crying. I didn't even flinch. Unthinking or without hesitation I drew my pistol blowing the top half of its skull clear off at close range. Amy jumped asking what had happened. Without any facial expression I simply told her it was nothing while gently pulling her forward by her hand.

## Chapter 3
## Retribution

-1-

It was even worse than we had any idea of knowing. We knew that Thomas and Kyle had likely not made it since they had only returned with Sam, but the horrid details of what had been done to them was beyond comprehension. The group as a whole was filled with an immense desire for retaliation. Whether it was to be defined as justice or revenge did not matter to any us. There was not a single person who elected to leave town or even suggested the idea. Jerod's death might have eventually been forgiven. It could have been a simple misunderstanding that led to death on both sides. After today there was no doubt that the only way this would end now was when we hunted down every single one of those sick fucks making them suffer before they died. Well, perhaps the suffering first was solely my thought, but I highly doubt I was alone in thinking it.

That night we doubled our original guard duty. Four of us and a dog stood watch throughout the night lost in our own individual thoughts. A couple days later Aurora was back to normal other than the stitches in her forehead of course. Kurt followed her around everywhere constantly asking if she needed anything or if there was anything he could do for her. Rye had been moving about in an arm sling ever since shortly arriving back at the airport. I had to threaten to tie him to a wheelchair if he wouldn't stop insisting on trying to take care of all the problems while pacing endlessly about the airport. I reminded him that there were plenty of capable intelligent people here that could handle some of the responsibilities. He laughed as if I were joking. I realize he feels the need to help. He is technically the leader of the group although no one would say it because he would outright deny it. Regardless he feels responsible for everyone and everything. Plus there is the fact that he is just a stubborn jackass sometimes. For all those reasons, I talked Dan into giving me some sleeping pills. I secretly dosed Rye with them so he could get the rest and healing that he needed.

The fact that we were still outnumbered was only a statistical factor to me. According to Aurora she was pretty sure none of them had any military training. A few had been avid hunters before the animal population had nearly ceased to exist, but most had never even handled a weapon up until the epidemic. What this meant is that a few were likely good with a gun, but they had no experience with tactics. This Preacher was the anomaly. He was not just dangerously insane, but also highly intelligent. Without him the rest would be unable to create a logical plan of attack or surmise proper courses of action. That being said, he was likely digging in or fortifying instead of moving on. He knew our group had to have a way to sustain ourselves or supplies to tide us over. He would not pass up the chance to take them if he could. After the blow we dealt him today, he would likely lay low for a while thinking of ways to inflict major casualties without direct contact. He would not needlessly sacrifice more of his men. With his way of thinking he was likely preparing more crosses for any of our party they could catch.

A week slowly crawled by. We buried Sam speaking words for all that were lost. Seeing how as the Preacher's group was low on supplies perhaps they chose to move on. It made logical sense being the alternative to starving. It also made sense being that it would simply be easier to acquire unprotected supplies than fight for whatever a group might have. However, they also could have found or taken a large stash from somewhere else.

Several more days passed making the likelihood seem more realistic that they had moved on. Being to weary to fight if it came would do none of us any good. We went back to two guards who now switched out every four hours to stay refreshed. We partnered up for all intents and purposes basically as couples now. Rye was the only one pulling double shifts with either Amy or myself. Technically Starlette and David had a third party member when they were on duty. To be honest I felt more secure knowing Tempest was on guard than those two put together. Not that they slacked in their duties, but because Tempest was more alert than most of us here. She was also as brave, cunning, and stealthy if necessary as the best of us.

The following day, as most had just sat down to share lunch, a call came over the hand-held radio. Dan and April were currently on guard detail. April let us know that a car was approaching slowly. We were quick to arrive on the scene ready for a fight. The car stopped about thirty feet from the newly erected barricades. A female got out standing beside the car with her hands raised in the air. Aurora recognized her as the woman she had previously mentioned to us by the named of Kate. Aurora and I exited the gated barricade taking a few steps forward while multiple guns were kept trained on her by the others.

"Aurora? Oh my heavens. Everyone thought you were dead. You being gone was one of the reasons I finally decided to leave. The other being that the Preacher has totally lost his marbles."

She lowered her arms starting to approach as if to give Aurora a hug. Knowing it would be awkward for Aurora, I lifted the muzzle of my own gun ordering her to halt. There was no way to know if she might have a bomb strapped to her or what her intentions truly were in that moment. Kate froze looking over to Aurora expecting her to come to her rescue.

"Just procedure Kate. I know you're a good person, but the others here don't know you at all. They have lost lives because of that sick bastard. Please just do what this woman tells you."

Kate nodded her head. I had her spin around while I patted her down checking for any hidden weapons on her person. She was completely clean.

"You may escort her inside now Aurora. We need to have a discussion with her prior to allowing her to move about the facilities freely. If you would take her to the room that you were originally a guest in, it would be much appreciated."

I handed her the key so she understood I meant for her to lock Kate inside for the time being. No matter how friendly this woman was it just seemed a little too convenient that she should show up out of the blue. Her story was too simple.

While Aurora escorted her inside I proceeded to search the vehicle top to bottom including underneath the car itself (in case there were explosives on the undercarriage). Knowing things could easily be hidden by someone with mechanics or body work knowledge I drove the car a good distance away from the airport just to be on the safe side.

Several of our group were huddled around the hallway as I approached the room where Kate was being held. Aurora stood in front of the door keeping guard while trying to answer questions about Kate to the others. It wasn't a scene like out near the hanger, but they were all apprehensive about having a member of the enemy being treated in such a well-mannered way.

"Alright everyone. Here is the deal. We will discuss what to do with her after I find out if she is a threat in any way. Just because she is not armed does not mean that she is not in some way a threat. I know some of you are not thrilled about having the enemy simply walk in. I want to remind you that Aurora was viewed as an enemy when she first came here as well. I have experience deciphering the truth. Please be patient until I'm through. That's all I ask. We don't need another incident like we had before, so please go back to doing whatever you were doing before this woman showed up."

A few in the group mumbled, but they all dispersed. Rye was the only one who remained. He told me to be careful and if I needed him that he would be waiting outside in the hallway. I kissed him on the cheek for worrying even though I could handle myself. In his condition if I somehow actually had a problem he would not likely be useful. I had Aurora unlock the door telling her to come inside with me. I presumed that having her as part of the conversation would be useful in determining facts or asking questions that I might otherwise overlook. Another reason was to give Kate the perception that we posed no threat so she would answer the questions that were asked.

'Hello, Kate. I'm Jessie. I apologize for any fright I may have given you prior and for the hospitality you have had so far."

"No problem, I understand. Things are not like they used to be anywhere these days. It's just how the world works. Very happy to see Aurora has been well taken care of. She always was kind to me."

"We have never turned others away. We have never harmed a person unless they intended us harm. Like you say the world has changed. Well, I guess we should try to get this over with if it's alright with you."

"Of course, I have nothing to hide. Anything you want to know I will do my best to answer."

"I suppose that since you are here it means that the Preacher has not moved on?"

"Sadly no. The Preacher moved everyone from the camp to a church across from city hall. There was a warehouse nearby that a search party found while out scouting. It had crates full of sealed snacks and junk food. He thought it would be easier to move close by the location than trying to remove everything they had found. The church was empty other than a few clergy that had turned. There are quite a few *Fallen* that roam about at night time in the streets though. One of the men got bitten while out in search of supplies. A few people got sick from a stomach bug due to some other food they found during that trip. Another important detail or what the Preacher referred to as the big score was the police station that was a couple blocks away. They acquired quite an arsenal, but lost a few men in the process. Art took care of most of the *Fallen* and put down anyone that got bitten."

"Art? Who is Art?"

"He is basically the Preacher's right hand. Whatever the Preacher wants Art supplies it. He follows the Preacher around like a lap dog," Aurora replied.

"Do you have any idea who killed our men leaving a couple nailed to crosses?"

"What? Seriously? I knew that crazy S.O.B. was losing it, but I can't imagine him being that gone in the head. I never heard anyone mention something like that. I did overhear about one of your guys. Supposedly a very large guy all muscles. They said he crushed Mike's face against a brick wall while they were trying to detain him. Supposedly one of ours stabbed him with a knife during the brawl, out of defense. Your guy somehow managed to escape on foot pulling a Houdini act."

"He was with two other men at the time. They are the ones who got crucified. When we found him he was barely alive. He didn't survive for long being pierced in a lung with apparently a knife. Whoever did it, twisted the knife to cause major damage and blood loss."

"Who were the ones you overheard talking about it Kate?"

"It was the two guys that came back from the airport by themselves. We all presumed everyone had died including you from the story we were told. They told us that during that evening while approaching the airport in search of food they were fired upon. When they got out trying to defend themselves several were shot by a sniper. They said that they just barely escaped being slaughtered with the rest. I believe the two men were Jasper and Art. One of the men was definitely Art."

"If all that you have heard about us have been atrocities, why exactly did you come here?"

"Because I know better than to believe everything I hear. I also know that all the men I heard these details from are avid liars. I have personally seen them do one thing, then claim to have done something completely different. I have seen them on multiple occasions outright kill someone claiming it to have been self-defense. While I don't know any of you for jack, I had nowhere else to go. As I said the Preacher has lost his marbles. I couldn't stick around for any longer."

"How so? You said he lost his marbles. What exactly caused you to finally leave?"

"Well, the new mandatory church service wasn't that big a deal I suppose. The offerings of food that were left at the altar was the first peculiar thing. Among other little things, the one that made me run was his idea of baptizing his flock in the blood of the *Fallen* after the altercation at the police station. He said it would protect everyone from being bitten or being inflicted with the Living Death epidemic in other ways. He also said it would empower them giving them wisdom from God. That was the final icing on the crazy cake for me. I secretly packed a bag sneaking out when I was sure no one else was paying attention. I stayed at a house with a for sale sign out front for a couple days before deciding to try my chances coming here."

"Sounds like quite the crazy cake indeed. If you don't mind Kate I would like to talk to Aurora real quick outside. I want to get her thoughts on everything."

"Yeah, no problem. Would one of you mind bringing me some water? I'm quite parched from talking so much. Plus I haven't had anything to drink all day. Ran out of water last night."

"Sure thing."

We stepped outside the room locking the door. Rye was standing nearby. We all walked to the restaurant taking a seat after making sure no one else was occupying it. I filled Rye in as we were walking.

"So, what did you make of that last part Aurora?"

"She isn't one to make up things normally, but to be honest Jessie it sounded like quite the whopper of a story to me. I'm not saying it isn't true. What bugs me though is why anyone would still be following him after that providing he truly is that far gone."

"I see you picked up on that obvious fact as well. Let's presume the story is false about the baptizing part. Did you believe everything else she had to say? And presuming the complete mental breakdown of the Preacher is false did she concoct the story herself or did someone feed the story to her? Is there anything they could hold over her to make her so blatantly lie? Regardless, she was sent here as part of a plan to get inside. Now we need to find out why."

"I hate agreeing with you. Out of everyone she is the one I would have least expected this from. The fact that the two of us were close means that obviously someone must know I am now part of your group. They used her to gain trust through me. So what do we do with her now? Should we question her until she cracks or just throw her out?"

"Seems to me that throwing her out would likely get her killed. I know you were close to her Aurora. Jessie told me that you have mentioned how persuasive this Preacher can be, but we need to find out what they are up to no matter the cost. Frighten her, torture her, I don't really care. I don't want to lose more of our group because we decided to simply do the easier of the two choices by throwing her out to be killed by her own people. If this Kate person really was close as you say, then I have no doubt you can get the truth out of her for her own sake," Rye said.

"You are of course absolutely right. I have an idea that just might work. Can you do a favor for me and find Kurt? I've become accustomed to him hanging about in my shadow. Not sure where he went off to."

"Probably hanging out with Dan somewhere. I'll go find him."

I grabbed a couple bottles of warm water off one of the counters. We patiently waited until Kurt arrived filling him in on the important details including what we were told had happened to Sam. He was delighted to know that Sam did not go down without a fight. The blood he had been covered in other than from the wound made sense now. Aurora told Kurt that the plan was to scare Kate while making her feel extremely guilty. She asked him not to hurt

Kate, just frighten her. If it progressed that far without the truth, I would take over from there. I explained this fact to Aurora so she would be prepared if it came to that point. I made it clear that no one would be able stop me from doing whatever was necessary to acquire the truth.

"You know what Jessie?"

"What Kurt?"

"You're kind of scary."

"Thanks, I will take that as a compliment. If I took it any other way I would have to hurt you."

I gave him a playful smile leaving my comment open-ended if I was actually joking or not. Even though it was Aurora's plan I sent her off to gather the others to fill them in on everything we had learned so far. I didn't want her to partake in the second interrogation as it would be easier to convince Kate we were sincere in our threats creating a better likelihood of fear. I explained that fact to Aurora who understood walking off without question. I unlocked the door stepping inside. We took seats across from Kate. Kurt handed her a bottled water.

"Seems Aurora had other matters to attend to. This is Kurt. He is one of the brothers of the guy that you mentioned earlier who got stabbed and eventually died."

"That's just what I overheard. I wasn't there, so no idea what actually happened. I told you those two men who I overheard are adamant liars. Hard to judge what parts of their conversation were actually true."

"Oh right, my mistake. Were you aware that the two men who were crucified and the one in the guard tower that was killed previously were all very close friends? Basically family?" Kurt continued to sit silently with his arms crossed giving her an angry glare while I spoke.

"I understand. You both have reason to hate and distrust anyone among the group that did those things. I'm sorry for your losses, but I had nothing to do with any of those deaths though."

"That is probably true Kate. However, the point is that you are dishonoring all of their memories which is almost just the same as if you had killed them!"

"How? What...do you mean?" Her eyes started to get big as she became suddenly worried that perhaps we were a little crazy like the Preacher.

"What I mean is you collaborated with the Preacher to come here. You are working for those that actually did murder our friends or family. I'm going to give you one more chance to make the right choice. After that all bets are off on what is going to happen to you in this room. Now let's try again. What were you sent here for?"

"No one sent me. I answered all of your questions. If you choose not to believe me then there is no point in trying to persuade you otherwise."

Kurt stood up. He reached out yanking the barely opened bottle of water from Kate's hand. He tossed the entire contents of the water in her face. Then he proceeded to crush the bottle with one hand into a lump of plastic before throwing it at the wall.

"How dare you be so disrespectful of what they did to my brother? Maybe you deserve to be dead like the rest of that lot!"

I could tell that Kurt was only acting even though he was pretty convincing. I'm sure part of it was simply venting true anger while keeping his mind focused. If only he had done that nights ago when Aurora first arrived. The reaction from Kate was as expected. A sudden immense fear turned into tears. I pulled out my knife sticking it into the table. She made a small scream nearly falling back in her chair out of fright. Her sobbing immediately ceased with her eyes bulging at the sight of the knife.

"As I said, last chance. We can do this the easy way or the hard way. Either way I promise I will find out the truth. I always do."

She didn't speak, only stared at the knife for a minute.

"Alright, you can leave Kurt. Looks like she wants to do it the hard way."

He went to the door starting to open it.

"No wait, wait! I'll tell you."

Kurt turned around with a slight look of relief on his face. He presumed I had every intention of using that knife to pry the truth out of her, but didn't want to believe I was capable of doing so.

"Glad you came around. Just so you understand clearly I will know if you lie even a little. If you make up another story I promise that no pleading will keep me from making you suffer. It will be twice as bad as what was about to happen to you if he had left the room."

I handed her the bottled water I had brought for myself. She took it with her hand shaking. Kurt pulled out a red mechanics rag from his back pocket for her to dry off her face with. It was almost like he had planned the scene with the water from the start. I removed the knife from the table sheathing it.

It took her a couple minutes, but she eventually opened the new water bottle taking a drink to quench her dry throat and calm her nerves.

"Everything I told you was basically true except the part about the Preacher wanting to baptize everyone with blood. I was supposed to find a way inside using Aurora to gain your trust. After that I was supposed to find out what kind of supplies you had. How much food, water, fuel, how many weapons, and other stuff that might be important. I was told to get a count on exactly how many of you were left, see if you had any routines outside the airport, or weaknesses that could be used."

"Did he ask you for a layout of the airport? How and when were you supposed to escape?"

"The Preacher already has blueprints of the airport from city hall. I was supposed to find a way to escape on my own. I was told to make my way to Harvey's Medical Supplies two weeks from today before sunset. He said if I betrayed him that he would kill all of you somehow without my help. Afterwards, he planned to chain Aurora to a wall after she turned. He was going to cut small pieces of me every day that would be fed to her while I was forced to watch. In the end he planned to set her free to let her devour what was left of me while I was still barely alive.

101

He isn't just crazy, the a-hole is psychotic. I knew that he had every intention of doing exactly what he claimed. I'm still afraid that he will if he succeeds in finishing off your group somehow."

"Why would he have you freely divulge his location? They are at a church across from city hall, right?"

"I don't know if it is part of a plan he has or if he just wanted me to be convincing. He told me to be absolutely truthful if questioned, but not to divulge why I was actually here. The part about the Preacher wanting to baptize everyone in blood was my own idea. It took me an entire day at the house I stayed at to come up with a way to make you believe why I would have left the other group."

"Thank you for finally being honest Kate. Neither of us wanted to harm you just so that you know. If I had not persuaded you to talk, I would have had no other choice though. I will send Aurora to check up on you in a little while. Make yourself comfortable. You will likely be locked in this room for a couple weeks. After that you will be free to go."

Kurt and I stood up to leave. Kurt of course had the impression that he should have the last word.

"Aurora says you're normally an honest person. You should have been straightforward with us in the first place. We would have protected you. This Preacher is bad news. The only place he is leading that flock of his is to a hell worse than the one we already have on Earth. Not telling us the truth could have gotten a lot more of our group killed. You understand that right? Just something to consider while you're enjoying your time with us."

We both left the room heading back to the restaurant area. Everyone had gathered patiently waiting for us to return. We filled them in on our last visit with Kate, since Aurora and Rye had already caught them up on the first conversation. Rye had a few thoughts about alternatives of what to do once two weeks had passed.

"There really is no easy answer. We could attack them before that time, but they are heavily armed. We could just not have Kate show up at their rendezvous in which case they will move on to whatever plan 'B' is. We can capture or kill the individuals that are supposed to meet her at Harvey's Medical Supplies. With that option we would eliminate more of their numbers. We could then possibly pose as them returning to the church which would require a plan of attack that wouldn't get us all killed in the process."

Unfortunately none of the plans were solid. None of them really accomplished much other than taking out one or two men for certain. I pondered what Rye had said for a minute before speaking.

"There is one other option we are overlooking. Harvey's Medical Supplies could be a trap that even Kate does not know about. It sounds like something the Preacher would devise. We already know he's smart even if the bastard is crazy. I suppose we could position someone in the area prior to their arrival with a radio. We would have to use code in case they are able to pick up the broadcast."

David brilliant as ever unwittingly gave me an idea with what he said after my response. "It's a start to a plan. We could have someone disable their vehicles. Maybe a sniper positioned to take them out if it's just a couple enemies. If it's not an ambush maybe we could take that rocket launcher back in whatever vehicle they bring. We could do some serious damage with that thing. Drive by rocket to the church perhaps?"

"That's it! In case I haven't said it lately, you're a genius. Only not so much with the drive by thing. Providing we can sneak into city hall, we should have the perfect position to end this once and for all."

"Sounds good to me. I realize you like the whole stealth thing Jessie, but I think everyone should go on this mission. All of us need to see this through to the end," Dan said.

"I couldn't agree more. After what they have done, everyone has a right to be present. Besides we are going to have to go at night, downtown, in an area that is apparently crawling with *Fallen.* The only way we are going to accomplish what needs to be done is as a group."

"We should probably take enough supplies and ammunition to last us for a few days just in case the plan goes sideways. There is always a chance something could go wrong. Better to play it safe than be sorry later," Aurora commented.

"We have to assume there is a chance that they are not at the church anymore or that telling Kate to be completely honest was to lure us in for an ambush. Let's hope they have not made their new permanent residence in city hall. Just to be certain, we need to scout the building outside and inside first thing on arrival. David see if you can find us a map of that area that shows all the structures in the vicinity. Kurt and Aurora you're both on weapons detail. Dan and April medical supplies. Amy and Starlette please handle the food and water. Rye and I are going to make a few slight modifications to our transportation.

Tempest, you should run around wagging your tail enthusiastically."

Tempest barked at hearing her name, which made everyone start laughing. I figured it would be a good way to break the tension including her in the plans.

April asked, "How long do we have to get things ready?"

"Very good question. Let's make it a week from today. That should be more than enough time."

-2-

When the following week finally came around everyone was on edge having to wait patiently for the day to arrive. We left enough rations for Kate to get by for a few days. We gave her the impression that we were going on a scouting trip for supplies outside of town. Around noon, we began loading all the supplies; making sure that there was not more than we could easily carry.

Rye and I had acquired two GMC Yukon SUVs with grill guards. We welded metal rods onto the guards after sharpening them down enough to easily impale anything in front of us. The glass was the challenging part. We found that instead of welding a ton of bars it was simpler to weld thin sheet metal over all the glass except the windshield. We used hinges to connect two pieces of the sheet metal together for both the front driver and the passenger windows so that they could fold open or closed as needed with latches to lock them if necessary. One of the extras we searched for when hunting for the SUVs was finding two that had removable sunroofs. On the roofs of the vehicles we mounted Gatling guns that could easily be operated with someone simply standing up from the back seat.

We had a decent small lunch consisting of peanut butter and apples from a small orchard farm about twenty miles outside of town. We left out around five in the afternoon. Our first destination was Hollinger Bank about fifteen blocks from city hall.

Most banks were shut down prior to the outbreak. It was a form of control that the government implemented as an attempt to force the people to calm down during the riots. That of course simply made the American dollar completely worthless in a matter of weeks. With other forms of monetization such as gold, ammunition, food, or gas; the banks basically became abandoned establishments that were left untouched.

Breaking in wasn't a problem with the power being down. Even the newer banks with the alarms that would still sound after the power was out were depleted of their back-up power sources by now. Once we unloaded the vehicles, we secured the doors from the inside with a couple large desks.

Come nightfall I had made my best attempt to camouflage the rest of the group. We already noticed a small number of *Fallen* creeping about outside. Waiting for the right moment we quietly loaded back up into the SUVs leaving behind some of the supplies to make the bank a secondary safe house if necessary. Starlette was the last to climb inside. She closed the door a little too hard. A few of the *Fallen* became aware of our presence due to the sound. They came at us just as we started the vehicles up. One ran slamming its head right into the door that Starlette had closed, just as we were taking off.

Two blocks away from city hall we pulled into an alleyway. Rye was at the wheel of the lead vehicle. He plowed down a couple *Fallen* before coming to a complete stop. Now parked, we were met by five more that came out of the shadows. Since the Gatling guns would make considerably too much noise Aurora stood up taking each of them out with her silenced pistol. We got out of the SUVs grabbing our supplies. Tempest was the last out of the Yukon that Rye had been driving. She started growling low at first then loud enough to catch a few of our attentions. Looking in the direction she was staring off towards no one saw the *Fallen* crouched in the shadows near a dumpster. Tempest shot off from where she had been standing with her teeth bared at some invisible foe that only she could see. Glowing blue eyes suddenly appeared mere inches away from April. Tempest slammed right into it knocking it backwards. It sprung right back up only to find that I had my gun pointed right at its temple. Slightly angling so the trajectory would not hit April I pulled the trigger at point blank. Blood and brain matter sprayed in April's direction covering her clothes and hair. She had protected her face with her arm just barely in time. She looked absolutely horrid covered in gore. The rancid smell made her dry heave until she actually lost her lunch. Amy gave her a bottle of water which she poured over her head trying to wash some of it off.

"I'm not sure if I should kiss you or kill you Jessie. Thanks, I guess."

Several of the others were quick to hide their smiles or choke down their laughter. We then made our way on foot from there. Making our way around the third side of city hall not facing the church we stopped at the side entrance. Kurt quietly broke one of the nearby windows after wrapping his shirt around the butt of his rifle. The falling glass on the concrete gave us a momentary concern for safety. We were extremely lucky that it didn't bring any unwanted attention. David hopped inside reemerging at the side entrance where he unlocked the door. We all entered locking the door back up. Inside the room with the busted glass we moved a file cabinet in front of the broken window. We then closed off the room's door just to be safe. I led the group since I had the only pair of night vision goggles. They used glow sticks to light their way behind me. We wanted to use as little light as possible so that we were not noticed from anyone over at the church, providing they were still there of course. We moved slowly, staying cautious of any potential threat. Luckily we knew that we could also rely on Tempest to warn us if we overlooked any potential danger. We progressed forward until we came to a set of nonworking escalators which we climbed to the second floor.

A door labeled City Attorney's office was the closest room which would be facing directly across from the church. We headed over to it cautiously keeping an eye on the several other rooms we passed.

"I'm surprised we have not run across any Fallen. Figured there would be a janitor or something," Dan joked.

Turning the handle of the City Attorney's door, Tempest started to growl low in her throat. I stepped back pulling out my knife.

"You had to say something didn't you Dan? No guns! We don't want a stray bullet warning anyone at the church that we are here."

Aurora came up beside me drawing a large survival knife. Rye grabbed a couple of the extra glow sticks that David and Star had been playing with. He tossed them in front of the door to give us some extra light. I gave Aurora a nod before flinging the door wide open. There were two Fallen inside the room barely wearing any clothing. Apparently, someone had been using the office for a secret affair even after the epidemic had begun to spread. At least that was the overall conjecture of the group after we put them down. Only one of them were wearing a wedding ring.

We rearranged some of the furniture to give us better defensive positions near the front windows. The light from the moon was more than enough for us to see by. We then barricaded the entryway into the room so we wouldn't have any surprises sneaking in behind us. We then sat around in the dark patiently waiting until the early hours of the morning. There had been illumination lingering on until around midnight. Now there was only one source of light that was visible. Looking through binoculars I saw it was a man walking around with a flashlight. He would disappear only to reappear up in the clock tower every twenty minutes while making his rounds. A few minutes after he had passed by the second time we busted out a couple windows which drew a small crowd of *Fallen* below us. The dead were beginning to swell in numbers walking about the streets by the time the guard came around again. He stopped standing in place for several minutes smoking a cigarette.

I lifted the rocket launcher aiming it directly at the clock tower. A second after pulling the trigger a huge explosion rocked the top of the church caving it downward. Aurora reloaded for me shortly after I fired the first time. I calmly redirected its projection at the main front doors. The instant I saw one of the doors start to open I pulled the trigger. The front half of the building exploded. The entire church was now set ablaze with a roaring fire. A large horde of *Fallen* began to swarm around the inferno. Several rushed through the flames intent on fulfilling their hunger from the corpses of those caught in the second blast. More would likely be heading this way from every direction in a matter of moments. A few of the Preacher's party apparently survived the onslaught. They broke out a side entrance attempting to mow down the small horde that blocked their path with gunfire. They were so preoccupied with the *Fallen* that they did not even consider the enemy that had destroyed the church.

There were three men in all who made their way through the horde with automatic weapons. They headed straight for a silver Honda Civic. Watching through the night vision goggles I saw one of the men made it inside the driver's side of the car. The other two men were quickly running out of ammunition becoming surrounded while the person inside the car was having trouble unlocking the passenger door. Focusing the goggles to zoom in I clearly saw that one of the men was wearing a cleric uniform like that of a Catholic preacher. The likely stolen attire was probably being worn by none other than the Preacher himself. Becoming almost completely surrounded by ever-growing numbers the man in the cleric uniform grabbed the other man shoving him towards the *Fallen*. This action gave him the time needed for the individual inside the car to unlock the door. He then jumped into the passenger door while the *Fallen* were ripping the man outside to shreds.

"Oh, I don't fucking think so!"

I grabbed the best sniper rifle we had. The silver car roared to life plowing down a few *Fallen* while backing up. It then sprung forward turning on the street to the left of city hall while swerving around as many of the horde as possible. I ran over to the window facing the side street busting in out before taking careful aim at the car. As it began to pick up speed I took my shot taking out the driver. He yanked the steering wheel to the right when the bullet pierced his chest. The car swerved striking the corner of a bail bonds building before flipping over on its side. A minute later the Preacher was pulling himself out through the side window which was now the highest point of the car.

*Fallen* quickly surrounded the overturned vehicle trying their best to reach the Preacher who was just barely out of their grasps. Everyone gathered around staring down from the window at what was taking place below. The street had filled up with at least a hundred Fallen pressing against each other in an attempt to get closer. The Preacher was yelling at them to stay back.

"This would probably be our best bet to get out of here. As long as they are distracted we have a chance of sneaking out the far side of the building."

The others nodded their heads and mumbled agreement. As much as we would have liked to watch the Preacher suffer immensely before he died; we all knew that this was our best chance of escaping. There was no way that the Preacher was going to be able to get out of the predicament he was in that any of us saw. We moved the desks from the entrance before heading down the escalators. Downstairs we made our way to the opposite side of the building finding a fire escape door that led outside.

-3-

As we headed back to the vehicles I couldn't help pondering if the Preacher would die of agonizing thirst or be ripped apart being devoured while still alive. April still somewhat covered in blood and gore was lingering behind the rest of us a bit, lost in her own thoughts. She wasn't paying attention and tripped on a pothole in the road. She went down banging up her knee pretty badly. Dan was intentionally holding back a bit waiting for her to catch up, but giving her space to contemplate her own thoughts. He heard her cry out in pain immediately turning around. A Fallen missing her right arm and a chunk of its torso lumbered out of the darkness attracted to the sound. It was literally standing over April a moment after Dan had turned. April covered her mouth while holding her breathe. Dan grabbed for his gun. The thing completely ignored April like she was invisible, but the movement from Dan caught its attention. It hobbled forward towards him with its teeth bared. A broken ankle slowed it down enough for Dan to get a good aim putting a bullet in its left eye. After it dropped to the ground he rushed forward to help April up from the street. She was having some difficulty walking due to injuring her knee. Without warning Dan lifted her off of her feet carrying her to catch up with the rest of us who had turned around after the silenced gunshot.

Having all the fun we could handle for one night, we loaded up making a quick stop at Hollinger just long enough to grab our supplies. As much as April smelled like rotted flesh and blood during the trip back to the airport no one commented unkindly. We all knew that for some reason that it was probably what saved her life according to what Dan saw transpire. It was useful information to have for the future if we ever needed it.

It was still dark out when we arrived back at the airport. It would probably be another three hours before the sun would start to rise. Most of us crashed immediately into a deep slumber. April stayed up to wash herself off. Dan patiently waited until she was finished so that he could tend to her knee. He helped her to her bed before retiring himself. When we awoke we were all so relieved that we could finally put all of this behind us that we took the day off. We relaxed while reading, playing cards, talking, and having a few alcoholic drinks to celebrate. Aurora and I went together to release Kate from her holding room. After explaining to her what had happened at the church, we gave her the choice of becoming part of the group despite her initial dishonesty. She made the choice to leave, feeling that she did not deserve the kindness we offered. As much as Aurora tried to talk her out of her decision it didn't help.

"I'm sorry Aurora. There's nothing else you can do. She's made her choice even if it isn't the best one. It's either let her go or keep her locked up indefinitely."

"I know. She won't make it out there on her own for long. I think she knows that."

"Could be, but it's not on you. You did everything you could to convince her. It's hard enough trying to keep the ones who want to live alive. They're the ones we have to look after."

Aurora nodded her head understanding as we watched Kate walk down the block until she was out of sight.

# Chapter 4
## Out of the Darkness

-1-

Around a month later we were attempting to get back to what was now considered a normal life even if others might view it as survival in a completely lost or overrun world. Whether *Fallen* or other survivors chose to make themselves our enemies; whether they killed our loved ones, it changed little. We would rebuild continuing to do our best holding true to our beliefs, morals, and the humanity that was left. We would hold those we lost within our hearts and minds dutifully paying them tribute with the memories we held of them.

One unparticular evening as a large part of the group was out searching for supplies, a sound came over the emergency band radio at the airport. I had been walking around nearby when I heard the faint noise following it back to its source. This radio had a secondary external power source. The only reason the secondary source had not been previously drained to our arrival is simply because it had been turned off all this time. David stumbled upon it not long after we arrived. He had messed around with it a few times, but had always found nothing other than silence. For some reason he had turned it on the night before completely forgetting to turn it off for the first time. I figured I must have simply heard some kind of static break which was the likely culprit of the noise I had heard. Reaching for the switch to turn it off a voice suddenly came over the line loud and clear making me slightly jump.

"If anyone is out there please respond. I am Peter Florence, one of the few that was in the neighboring cities when the explosion first created the *Fallen*. I'm currently located in Alpine, Texas. The northern lights are quite extraordinary in the mountains this time of year. I have seen quite an immense amount of wildlife despite the circumstances. We have started a small colony that is protected from the *Fallen*. We have power, water, and a source of food from crops that are growing immensely. We are looking for others that would like to contribute to our society with one goal in mind. That goal is simply to restore humanity while protecting each other from harm."

As sincere as the whole speech came across I could not let myself believe that there was a colony of survivors that had accomplished so much. I had learned in my younger days pretty quickly that when something sounds too good to be true it usually is. Without being able to see his gestures or facial expressions all I had to go off of was the pitch of his voice. As much as I argued with myself that this was a hoax or trap, I heard no nuances that told me he was lying either. Even if what he said was true we were doing alright for ourselves for the time being. *Fallen* were somewhat manageable while out searching during the daytime as long as we stayed away from the heavily populated areas. The truth is that the living outside our small community were the greatest threat aside from the hordes of *Fallen*. Even if this Peter was a good guy, it didn't mean everyone is his colony were. Regardless of my own disconcertion the choice was not mine to make alone. I picked up the mic pressing down the button to talk.

"Mr. Florence. Good to hear another voice out there. This is Colonel Jessie Sparks previously of the Marine Corp. How are you doing today?"

"Doing even better now that I hear a new voice out there alive. So you were with the military? Mind switching over to a more private channel? Say thirty-five perhaps?"

I changed the channel to the one requested.

"Mr. Florence you there?"

"Yes ma'am. Was just waiting for you to respond so I could make our conversation a bit more private. This channel was hardly ever used by anyone other than citizens, plus using a scrambler should help for any prying ears"

The moment I heard his voice I clicked a switch that said private. A radio like this would have come in handy back in Ruidoso. It would lock in a signal with the person incoming over the air making it impossible for outside ears to hear any conversation that I broadcast. From that point it would sound like this Peter fellow were having a conversation with himself.

"Why the secrecy?"

"Well, the thing is Colonel that there are several in our group including myself that have issues trusting the military for obvious reasons. We are just taking the precaution in the possibility they may still be an organized threat. Might I ask if you have any information pertaining to ground zero of the Living Death?"

"Jessie or Mrs. Sparks is fine if you prefer. To be completely honest, I have absolutely no information regarding ground zero. I was outside the U.S. when it occurred only seeing what was made public by the media. I have very recently had a falling out with upper brass. It is highly likely that I could even be on the former President's personal hit list."

"Seriously? I would very much like to learn the details of how you managed to find yourself in such a predicament with a government that has all but vanished as far as we knew. I also think it wise to fill you in on all the details of what actually occurred back on day one. Seeing everything first hand is only part of it. There is plenty of information to support what actually happened based on knowledge and facts, but there is nothing completely concrete that would hold up in court, providing we still had those."

"Sounds like we both have pertinent information to share with each other."

"I completely agree! I suppose you heard my broadcast about our community. If you're interested in joining I guarantee your past military affiliation will be expressed in an exuberant light to the others. Or if you preferred it be kept secret except between yourself and those that can manage dealing with the truth in a proper manner, I'm sure that could be arranged."

"I appreciate the offer Mr. Florence. I am part of a larger group. It is not a choice I can simply make on my own. We will have to discuss the matter when they are all available. There is one other with us that also has a military past. She served four years in the Army Reserves to support her education. She was nothing more than an up-and-coming author right before the emergence of the Living Death. What I want to know Mr. Florence is if protecting our country is really a problem for your group, because it sounds like it is. If willingly volunteering to sacrifice our lives to protect our nation, the citizens, and their rights is wrong...then I can guarantee not one single person in our group would be willing to join your community. It might matter if we lived in a barren desert and you had all the water, but that's not the case. We would rather die than conform or admit fault for doing our best to serve our country."

"I apologize Mrs. Sparks for giving the wrong impression. I clearly came across the wrong way previously. I understand that not all parts of any group or affiliation have the same like-mindedness. I did not mean to express that the entire military or those that served were like a plague worse than the Living Death. I'm simply bad at saying what I mean to actually say. There are plenty of veterans as well as previously active military that are part of our group. It's hard to know which side a person falls on or what they stand for without asking questions that might seem offensive. It's also hard to have trust without building it first. There were a great number of the government and several within the military who handled things in a bad light. It is my personal impression that they even caused the virus which led to the world we now live in. However, I should not sound like I am stereotyping all that fall under those groups. Please forgive me for coming across the wrong way with my words."

"Peter, I do have to say you need to work on those social skills. However, the way you went about testing my allegiance was pretty clever. If what you just said is actually true about the government creating the virus then I can understand the mistrust you likely have. There are good and bad people everywhere, we all make mistakes, and we all lost loved ones due to this plague. Everyone is affected by the Living Death. Every living person has to fight to survive from the *Fallen* despite who or what they did before it all began. We have to work together if there is ever going to be a future."

"You have a special way with words Mrs. Sparks. I mean Jessie. You gave me a different perspective on how I should perhaps express myself. It is true that I was testing you, but I admit that due to the things that happened to myself and others that day there is likely also lingering resentment that is probably clear to the right ears listening. As you say, it would no doubt be more constructive to work together or there will be no future. I apologize again if I offended you or degraded the sacrifices most of the men and women of the military have made. It is nice to talk to someone that expresses themselves so genuinely in such a straight forward manner."

"Glad to hear. Now that is out of the way, back to what I was saying before. I will have to discuss the situation with the others. However, I would like to meet with you regardless of what is decided. Is it possible to meet somewhere between Alpine and El Paso?"

"El Paso? Don't tell me you are in one of the big cities?"

"No, of course not.  We also have some trust issues to be honest. Only difference is ours is with the human race in general. I feel safer not giving away our location. And since we are being honest, if we meet then I will be bringing armed men for my protection. I'm sure that your experiences with others have not all been rainbows since the explosion either Mr. Florence. It is only the intelligent, the cautious, and unfortunately those that have done unspeakable atrocities that still survive in the new world."

"Too true Jessie. Hmm, how about Kent? Let's say a week from now? That is a middle ground from the area

125

you described. A week should give your group some time to think about the proposal before we meet."

"Let's say just west of the city limits on the highway so it will be easier to locate each other. We can figure out somewhere safe to go from there if need be."

"That will work. Sometime around lunch sound good? We will bring fresh bread and a nice bottle of wine."

"Sounds perfect as long as you eat and drink some first of course."

He laughed before speaking again. "No problem there, but once I get started I might not stop. See you soon Jessie."

I shut off the radio to save whatever juice it might still have before returning back to my roaming of the airport. When the others made it back I filled them in on the conversation with Mr. Florence. Most of their initial responses were the same as mine had been prior to talking to Peter. After hearing the entire discussion I had, everyone shared the same small hope that maybe just this once it really was true without a catch.

It was decided that Kurt, Dan, and Tempest (whom Starlette volunteered) would be making the trip along with me. Hearing Tempest would be traveling along reassured me that things would go smoothly or at least in our favor if things went bad. She was as good at reading people as I was, probably even better. If she sensed a threat she would be on them before they even realized it.

-2-

The week passed slowly as we continued our normal routine. It was decided that we would leave the day before to make sure we were not walking into a trap of some kind. When that day came we packed up the few things we needed in Rye's RV for the trip. We said our goodbyes before hitting the road. It was the first time any of us openly saw Dan kiss April, telling her he would make it back safely. If we had not returned by the day after tomorrow the rest of the group would assuredly come hunting for us despite any potential danger. Those of us going knew there was little we could say to sway them. In their positions we would do the exact same thing for anyone else in what we considered our family.

A few hours later, we came to the Kent population sign. We slowed down making a U-turn. About a quarter mile back we had passed a Travel Stop (tourist center and gas depot). We headed back to it since it was the best option for the meeting. Tempest was happy to be able to run around after being cooped up in the RV. She dashed outside the second I opened the door. We made a quick sweep of the place finding only two *Fallen* inside (a clerk and a customer). The Weatherford brothers siphoned gas refueling the RV. I made a decent size sign from supplies I found inside the Travel Stop. The sign said 'Mr. Florence' with an arrow below his name (all of which was written in a bright lavender marker). I set it under a windshield wiper of an abandoned car on the highway facing towards Kent. The arrow pointed directly over to the Travel Stop. We gorged ourselves on candy and chips long past there expiration dates from vending machines set up near the restrooms. Borrowing a deck of cards with half nude women on them and poker chips from the tourist gift section of the Travel Stop; we sat down to play Texas Hold'em to pass the time. Dan ended up beating the both of us. His poker face was impossible for me to read and there was no expression or movement of any kind when he was bluffing. Kurt informed me that Dan always made playing games no fun because he never lost at anything growing up. Kurt was happy to find a large stash of various cartons of cigarettes. Seems he was a chain smoker prior to the epidemic, but had to quit due to the shortage it created. Since neither Dan nor I were fond of cigarette smoke so he went outside smoking an entire pack before returning light headed with a smile on his face.

As the evening continued, the sun followed its course across the sky. When it neared the horizon, we were just considering if we should retire early (taking turns on guard duty). Being the end of September the sun was now setting around nine at night. Kurt and I were just unrolling sleeping bags when Tempest barked followed by Dan banging on the roof with the butt of his rifle. We grabbed our guns stepping back outside.

A large black car with its headlights already on prior to sunset was heading towards us from the direction of Kent. As it got closer we saw it was a limousine of all things. It slowed down a pace as they spotted us standing at the ready armed for any confrontation. The driver slowly pulled up next to the RV stopping next to it. The very back window lowered revealing a man with short brown hair and brown eyes. He was wearing a thin pair of glasses. He stuck his head out the window with a goofy grin on his face.

"Mrs. Sparks, I presume?"

"The one and only."

"Seems we had the same after thought of arriving early in case it was a trap. Apparently, you bested us on making it here first. Unless you have a large party in hiding I suppose my concerns were unwarranted."

"There could be a large party hiding in the RV or the Travel Stop, but you'll have to take my word that there is not. I would not compromise the safety of my entire group over the formality of a first meeting. Besides if either those you're with or those with me were to go missing then you realize others would assume the worst responding in a manner that could cost many lives."

"Nicely chosen words. I would expect nothing less after our previous conversation. Well, seeing how it is already late I do not wish to overstay my welcome. We need to get some rest ourselves. Saw a small estate just inside Kent that we will head back to for the night. We can continue our conversation as planned tomorrow if that's alright?"

"Works for us. Be careful of the *Fallen*. Would hate to wait all day tomorrow only to find you were eaten or turned. I'd seriously not like for your party back in Alpine to get the wrong first impression if that were to happen."

"Ha, no worries. We can handle a few Fallen. Keep safe yourselves. See you tomorrow morning."

The window rolled back up as the limo turned around heading towards the direction of Kent. We waited another hour before attempting to go to sleep. Kurt traded guard duty with Dan around four in the morning. Kurt should have woke me up by eight, but instead it was closer to ten that I was awoken by a rooster somewhere in the vicinity. I exited the RV finding Kurt relaxing in a lounge chair.

"Why didn't you wake me up Kurt?"

"Sorry lost track of time reading 'Deadheads' this whole time."

"Aurora's book? Any good?"

"Actually it is very detailed with some coincidental similarities to everyday life we have had to deal with ever since the Living Death came about. The Deadheads are close to the *Fallen* we have roaming around, but they all seem to have a really high intelligence level. She went with red glowing eyes probably to make them seem evil or scarier I suppose. The whole thing is pretty trippy. It's almost like reading another person's diary. I'll let you read it when I'm finished if you're interested. Oh, check this out."

He opened the book to the inside front cover. Aurora had autographed it. She wrote, 'To Kurt, Thanks for sharing Armageddon with me. I know you'll always have my back like George and Carla do in the book. You're a great friend to have in the dark times ahead. Watch out for those Deadheads and stay safe! Aurora Whitaker.'

I held in laughter at the fact that Kurt had gotten her to sign it. In the normal world it would have increased the value by twice if not more depending on just how popular she became. Now it was kind of a silly saying between friends. At the same time it obviously would be a nice keepsake and priceless to Kurt."

"That was nice of Aurora. I'll have to get her to personalize a copy for me when I come across one."

Dan stepped out of the door I had left open. He looking around stretching.

"I take it that bloody rooster woke you up too Dan?"

"Yeah, if you see it be sure to shoot it twice. Once for waking me up and another for being so damned annoying."

"Will do. Kurt didn't wake me up for guard duty. He was too busy reading his girlfriend's book which she autographed for him."

"Girlfriend? When did this happen? She autographed your book? Let me see!"

Kurt held out the book for Dan while slightly blushing. Dan smiled as he read Aurora's words.

132

'Well, I said girlfriend, but he still has made his move. When are you planning on doing that Kurt? It's not like you're getting any younger you know."

"I do like her very much and she is gorgeous as hell. I'm just not great with words to express my interest I suppose."

"You Weatherford men are huge clouts when it comes to women. Luckily, Dan finally got his act together. It's not like you have to find the most eloquent words or perfect opportunity. Just go for a walk, ask her to have lunch alone with you, or something simple. When the time is right, kiss her. Everything else will fall in place. She'll probably be the one doing most of the talking anyway."

"You really think she likes me?"

"Yes, Kurt. If it were any more obvious it would smack you in the face."

"Alright, I'll think of something before Rye snags himself a third female."

"Hilarious, Kurt. Try not to be a knucklehead when you talk to her. You'll likely end up on your backside tending to a head wound instead of the way you intended to end up there."

Dan commenced to laughing hard. Kurt tried to keep his composure, but was soon laughing himself.

A couple hours passed before the second arrival of Mr. Florence's limousine. He stepped out wearing an expensive white suit with a purple striped tie. He was also wearing a white cowboy hat and alligator boots dyed white. On his left breast pocket he had a small Texas flag pinned to it.

"Trying to make yourself feel more like a Texan? You realize most Texans actually don't dress up like cowboys, don't ride horses, and you can't even tell from their accent that they are from Texas right?"

"I realize that it is a common misconception, especially to foreigners. Haven't actually ran across any *Fallen* or otherwise as of yet. The thing is I always wanted to be cowboy when I was younger. Now here I am living in Texas. Couldn't find a white horse unfortunately."

"You are quite the character Peter. How about we get down to business. That's provided you're still good for the bread and wine of course."

Peter laughed as three others stepped out of the limousine carrying a bottle of wine and a covered basket which I assumed was the bread. He introduced his associates as Kim, Charles, and Richard. He tapped on the roof of the limo before another female stepped out of the driver's door. He told her to join us stating she was his daughter Celeste from Wyoming. Tempest came out from under the RV startling Peter's group momentarily. I assured them that she was safe provided their intentions were good. Tempest sat down looking each of them over. The women in Peter's group drew closer fawning over her with attention that Tempest rather enjoyed.

So that we were not all standing around, I suggested that we converse inside the Travel Stop lounge area. Once inside we relayed the details of our personal stories. Peter was quite surprised to learn about the former President reinstating project Raven Storm and what it was capable of. He told us that it was not a nuclear reactor that exploded. Of that I had no argument telling him that there were no known nuclear reactors even in that vicinity (including top secret ones) to begin with. He stated that he knew some government employees that worked at the building that actually exploded for several years. Prior to it happening, they privately informed him on more than one occasion after having a few too many drinks that the place was a top secret military facility dealing with biological warfare, genetics researching, and other things they were not even aware of. He went into detail of everything that happened directly after the explosion, finishing with how he barely managed to sneak past the military barricades more out of luck than anything.

Trying not to be aggressive I carefully nudged him into discussing the colony. I was most interested in the protection it had, how big the population was, and what kind of skills they possessed. Peter was elated to discuss his achievements. I say 'his achievements' only because he spoke as if they all came about due to his direction. He had been elected by the group unanimously to lead for a four year term with a provision that allowed the group to remove him from office for any reason through a majority vote.

Peter informed us that there were around seventy people that had gathered together from various cities and states. He described multiple ways he used to get the word out. He said there hasn't been a single day that has passed without looking for more survivors. His intention was to save as many lives as possible. He told us that at first it was near impossible to sustain supplies when the group started growing. Among the people that trickled in were previous city employees, electricians, ranchers that dealt with crops and livestock, and other prevalent individuals that had knowledge to get a community up and running. He said the problems of food, water, electric power, and others were quickly solved. He explained that everyone in the community had jobs, knew how to defend themselves as many raiders found out the hard way, and that defenses were well maintained.

As far as defenses they started off with a small area fenced in with around the clock guards. That small area grew over time. There had been a nearly year-long project of putting up cyclone fencing and clearing *Fallen* around different portions of Alpine that facilitated important needs such as residential neighborhoods for living space, areas rich in soil to grow crops, a hunting area that actually still has a variety of wild animals roaming about, and other things. He said one of the major areas was a business district that is home to a school, medical facility, and a place to trade goods or services with other in the community. After all the hard work they had done supposedly the *Fallen* population was pretty minimal in the vicinity. The only time they really faced any danger from them now was while going scouting the surrounding cities for supplies. According to his philosophy, the seclusion of Alpine made it less likely new Fallen would travel the long distance through the rough terrain.

Almost everything he said sounded hard to believe, but I did not detect he was lying. Tempest herself seemed to find Peter trustworthy as she constantly begged him to pet her.

"It is a lot to take in. It would be a huge change from what we have become accustomed to for the last couple years. My instincts and military experience tell me to trust you. That being said, we are made up of a small group that has for a while now lived at an airport. We have good defenses, a greenhouse, and Fallen stay away for the most part. They tend to stay in the city whether it's habitual or some other reason. The recent confrontation I lightly mentioned was that of a larger party which costed the lives of several people close to us. The fact we are rather shorthanded or outnumbered is a problem. Even though we are more than capable of handling ourselves or taking care of our own, there are a few reasons why we have seriously considered your offer. One being there is safety in numbers of course. Another is that we have always had a similar goal of building a large community in hopes of eventually reclaiming everything this epidemic has taken from us; while at the same time saving every life we could. I suppose the last reason being that if what you have said is true then you're already several leagues ahead of what we have accomplished. I think we might have been halfway to where you are now provided we had not had to deal with the military presence in New Mexico that made us start all over again. Regardless, we are still simply considering the offer. It really is going to depend on other factors not yet discussed."

"I understand the difficulty of change. We have all endured dramatic and overwhelming hardships since the epidemic began. However, this is a good change. You have had challenging trials that have rightly created doubts of everything I have told you. Despite those doubts, you are willing to trust me enough to share information about your own group that some might perceive as a weakness. I think the ability to show trust is a strength that few still have in the world we live in. At the same time I'm pretty sure you are confident enough in your group's skills and abilities to believe you can overcome anything together. That is something I find highly admirable. We do honestly have a lot to offer. I truly hope you will consider becoming part of our community. You would no doubt be great assets in helping us achieve mutual goals we both desire. Together I believe we really can eventually can take back this country even if it takes generations to do so."

"To be completely honest Peter we could continue discussing a large number of topics for days without coming to a decision one way or the other. The thing that is going to make or break our decision would involve actually visiting Alpine firsthand, so we could see for ourselves what it is like."

"That can be arranged for any time you would like. We have nothing to hide as you will find for yourself. Just notify anyone you find when you arrive that you are there to see Peter Florence. I'm not one to believe in titles even though many have been suggested. My name alone has always been good enough for me."

-3-

We talked for a couple more hours while sharing bread and wine. We eventually said our goodbyes as we went our separate ways. We returned to Salt Flat later that evening. Tempest was overjoyed to see Starlette again. She barked happily running around in circles until she tired herself out. Everyone greeted us overjoyed that we safely returned. Over a dinner of vegetable soup made fresh from the garden, we discussed our trip in detail. They were excited with the details we relayed. The fact that both Tempest and I felt no malice or distrust in those we met gave them hope. We all agreed that it would be a good idea to take Peter up on the visit to Alpine before making a final decision. Leaving the airport unguarded was however not an option. Until we were a hundred percent certain about the move; the airport could never be undefended. Choosing who would make the trip to Alpine was extremely difficult seeing how absolutely everyone wanted to go. We came to a decision that five could go leaving five behind. Tempest was the first chosen to stay behind as she would be a greater protection here (plus she didn't argue in her own defense about having to stay). Dan was chosen to stay behind simply because if someone got injured or sick his skills would be invaluable. Peter's group likely had someone with medical experience since he mentioned the clinic in the business district. Dan wasn't thrilled, but he acknowledged that the reasoning was sound. The thought of Tempest staying behind for an extended period of time took its toll on Starlette over the next couple of days. She willingly volunteered to stay. David shortly followed suit wanting to be near Star. During our initial discussion the group originally thought Rye should stay behind because he was basically the leader. His safety was viewed as a high importance to the majority. While discussing that fact, Dan pointed out that Rye's input from directly experiencing Alpine himself would be extremely valuable in making a serious decision on relocation. Rye was immediately voted as the first to be making the trip after everyone considered the fact Dan pointed out. I was chosen as the second to go because I had more communication with Peter than anyone. My skills in finding anything that might be amiss was the other reason. Amy was volunteered by the group because of her relationship with Rye and myself. Plus her brothers knew that she would be pissed at them if they didn't let her go with us. April was the fifth that chose to stay since Dan wasn't going. That left Kurt and Aurora with us on the to-go list.

It took a few more days to get in touch with Peter over the radio. We let him know that a few of us would be making the trip at the end of October. Even though he had left an open invitation it just seemed the more respectable thing to do. He told us to let the ones being left behind know that we would be return bearing gifts for everyone so that they did not completely feel left out.

Around the twenty-fifth snow began to fall. The weather is Texas is always anything except predictable. It can change from sun to snow in the same day. On this occasion the snow continued for three days straight. Luckily it was half way melted by the time to leave came around. With the roads still somewhat unsafe it was going to take twice as long to drive to Alpine. Rye told the others to turn the radio on around five each evening. He said that we would do our best to contact them every day, but if they didn't hear from us by five-thirty to turn it off to conserve the energy. We found some snow chains for the RV tires before officially leaving Salt Flat early in the morning on the thirty-first.

Alpine was about a hundred-sixty miles away. It took us six hours to get there. Not long after arriving we came across one of the cyclone-fenced areas. We were greeted by a couple of friendly, but cautious faces. They asked who we were. After expressing that we were there to see Peter, they became much friendlier. Apparently everyone had been told to be expecting us sometime today according to the conversation we had with these individuals. Two of the five we came across loaded up in a four-wheel drive truck telling us to follow them. They led us to an immense rural area completely surrounded by fencing. A guard tower stood erected on the inside of the enclosed area. Two men on the inside pulled open a large pair of gates after being honked at by the men in the truck. They closed them right after we entered. They had to walk over to a second set of gates that opened up to the residential housing after verifying that the men in the truck were under no duress.

We followed the truck several blocks before turning off on a street called Nightingale. A third of the way down the street smoke poured from the chimney of a nice quaint little house. The decorations in the yard were very appropriate being that it was Halloween. The fact that it was Halloween had basically escaped most of our minds being that we had not celebrated it in a long time. The only holiday we actually did observe was Christmas. It was more specifically a time to rejoice that we were still alive with alcohol and good company.

The two men in the truck shouted this was the place before waving as they drove away. We all got out stretching our legs. Rye was the first to arrive at the threshold of the front porch knocking lightly. Peter answered the door dressed as a lumberjack wielding a bloody axe. The response from everyone was one of surprise. I admit that I reached for my pistol momentarily before recalling that it was Halloween.

"Umm, trick or treat?" Rye smiled hoping to not give the impression we had been startled.

Peter must have noticed from one or more of us that we had been slightly edgy for a moment. "Sorry if I gave anyone a fright. We don't get a lot of new visitors on holidays. Anyone want some candy?"

"Think we will pass on the candy for now," I said. I then commenced to make introductions to Peter of those he had not previously met.

He invited us in his house which was filled with fake spider webs, eerie strobe lights, and other decorations. Peter shut off the strobe light seeing the strange looks he was given for having them on when it wasn't even close to dark out. There was also a CD player bantering out spooky noises. Peter was very much into the spirit of celebrating Halloween to its fullest. We found out later the reason for this was because among the population there were seven children under the age of twelve. The community as a whole wanted to pass on the various holiday traditions so that they were remembered generations from now. I suppose it was a bit ironic being that everyday life was now more terrifying than Halloween. It was still nice to later see the children dressed up in costumes.

Peter set his axe near the front door before turning down the music. He told us to make ourselves comfortable. We did so by lounging around on the sofas in the large living area. We had some small talk about the weather and our drive here. Peter gave us a tour of his house, which he had put a lot of work into remodeling himself. He then apologized for being a bad host asking if anyone would care for a refreshment. He said that he had cold beer, tea, and water. He also stated that there was plenty of ice if we preferred any of those beverages on ice. This alone amazed us enough to revisit his kitchen after the tour. He then asked if anyone would like eggs or spaghetti for lunch. Both sounded delicious especially the eggs which I had not had in forever. Helping out a little in the kitchen we ended up making both for lunch. Peter didn't seem to mind in the least.

After our late lunch we relaxed at the dining table conversing a little about Alpine. As five in the afternoon rolled around Rye politely asked if he could borrow Peter's radio to contact the others back at the airport. He informed him that we had promised to try to contact them every day if possible that we were gone providing it was not a problem. Peter was more than happy to oblige showing Rye to his study room.

"It's not the one I use to make daily broadcasts, but works just as good."

Rye thanked him before having a seat at a desk with the radio sitting on it. Peter left him alone unworried that his things might be rifled through. In the kitchen, Kurt stood up from the table holding his stomach with one hand. He looked over at Aurora who smiled affectionately.

"I need to walk all that food off. Would you like to go for a walk with me Aurora? Maybe check out the neighborhood?"

"I would love to go for a walk."

She stood up excusing herself from the table. Amy and I both smiled as they went out the front door.

"About time he gets with the program."

Amy laughed in agreement. She wanted both of her brothers to be happy. She also very much approved of Aurora unlike with April who took much convincing. We both got up moving near the fireplace in the living room since it was a little bit chilly. We relaxed cuddling on a couch until Rye returned. When he returned finding us in the living, we scooted apart making room for Rye. We snuggled up with him to keep warm after he sat down. Peter who had been sitting on a nearby sofa appeared a little surprised, but did not touch the subject. Instead he commenced to letting us know that the other houses on the block were allocated as guest houses for new arrivals until they found sufficient residence elsewhere. He stated that the longest anyone had stayed in one of the guest houses was around a month. Apparently, it took some convincing to get that particular couple to part with the guest house for a permanent residence elsewhere because they had grown fond of it. I suggested that is must get lonely living on an entire block by himself. He said it could be at times, but he preferred the quiet solace too. He admitted it was part of the reason that he made such a huge deal out of the holidays. Greeting everyone and socializing during such times made it more tolerable the rest of the year. Plus his daughter came to visit at least once a week if not more.

A little while later Kurt and Aurora returned. Aurora was absolutely glowing with a huge smile on her face. Amy and I snuck her off with the excuse we were going to clean up the kitchen. The men protested saying they would do it. We convinced them we were going to do it tactfully to make sure they did not suggest helping. Once in the kitchen we pried the details out of her that we already pretty much figured had happened. After walking a little while Kurt had suggested the stop to sit on a bench swing in front of one of the houses. Eventually he got up the courage to kiss her which led to more passionate kissing. After hearing all the details we finished up what we hadn't cleaned while talking before returning to the living room. The men were standing around waiting near the front door. Peter explained he was going to show us to a guest house so we could unpack our things. He led us across the street to a decent sized house. Pulling out a ring full of keys he rummaged through them to find the right one. He took it off the ring handing it over to Rye.

"Electricity, tap water, and gas work. I'm sure you will likely fight over who gets the first hot shower like most do. Luckily there are two bathrooms which should make it a little easier. Unfortunately one has a shower and the other a bathtub."

"Seriously? Am I dreaming? If so don't anyone wake me up!"

"Amy, right? It is not a dream fortunately. Took a lot of hard work, but all utilities really do work. Make yourselves at home. The thermostat is set at seventy-six degrees. Feel free to adjust it as you like. The closets are full of different sizes and styles of clothing for both genders. You are welcome to whatever you fancy. The washer and dryer also work if you have become attached to your own clothing. You are more than welcome to stop back over at my place once you have settled in. Pretty sure a few people will be dropping by if you're up to meeting a few new faces."

We thanked Peter moving the RV across the street to unload our things. Amy was first to dart off to take a shower. After she had finally finished, everyone else was being courteous enough to offer letting others take a shower before them. Standing around talking, Kurt suggested that Aurora should take the next shower if she wanted. Aurora jumped on the suggestion grabbing Kurt's shirt by the collar pulling him along behind her. She shut the door behind them locking it.

"I guess all that pent up attraction for each other finally got the best of her. No telling how long it has been for either of them. Can't say I wouldn't have done the same exact thing," Amy said.

"Oh really? Can't say I recall you inviting Rye or me when you took off to have the first shower."

Amy gave us a sad face. She apologized saying that the thought hadn't even crossed her mind or she would have. I had been giving her a serious look like it really bothered me. I finally cracked a smile.

"I was just joking Amy. You didn't hurt either of our feelings in any way beautiful. Plus there is always tomorrow," I said while giving her a wink.

After everyone had showers, we raided the closets. Showering, shaving, and now wearing new clothes the lot of us looked like we had just stepped out of the 'Twilight Zone' into a dimension where *Fallen* ruled the planet. We returned to Peter's house wearing our new attire. There was a man with a little girl dressed up as a princess standing at his front door. Peter waved us over making introductions. The little girl named Stephanie was seven years old. She was the cutest sight I had seen in several years. At first she was pretty shy hiding behind the man named Roger. She finally found the courage to greet us. Before they both left she ran up to me asking for a hug. I did not realize I had made an impression on her until that moment. They both waved bye as they left.

We met several other people that stopped by just to meet us. All the other children in the community came by dressed in costumes over the following hour to get candy. Peter told us that most of the children had been rescued early on by different people. Some of them had undergone traumatic experiences. Most had at some point lost their parents and close relatives. They were brought in by those who had rescued them only to be handed off for the community to figure out what to do with them. Luckily there were many volunteers that wanted to welcome them into their homes. There were actually an overwhelming number of volunteers making placement somewhat difficult. The volunteers that the children were placed with eventually made them permanent parts of their families. The whole thing was sad, but uplifting to hear. It made even the toughest of us almost want to shed a tear in the beginning. We all had huge smiles by the end of his story. Peter told us that there were festivities going on if we were interested. We excitedly agreed to partake in the community festivities. We followed him in the RV to a barn that was fully decked out for Halloween. There were too many people we met to recall even half of their names. They actually bobbed for apples which I had never before witnessed except in perhaps cartoons growing up. There was a lot of talking, dancing, and drinking. There was a table fully adorned with various desserts. Pumpkin pie always has been my favorite dessert any time of the year. One of the women saw how much I loved the pie promising to bring a freshly baked one just for me the following day.

We eventually returned to the guest house. Kurt and Aurora stayed up watching horror movies on a Blu-ray Player into the wee hours of the morning while the rest of us retired from the long day.

## Chapter 5

## Living Nightmare

-1-

Dan had taken guard duty the first night we were gone. April tossed and turned thinking about Dan. She eventually got up after a couple hours of restlessness joining him for the remainder of the night. They wrapped themselves in heavy blankets to keep warm.

Once Star and David had awoken they told the grown-ups that they should get some rest. Dan asked if they were sure they would be alright by themselves. They replied that they would be perfectly fine. He headed off to get some sleep with April following close behind. She insisted that she needed to snuggle up with him to actually get some sleep. Dan did not object in the least. Even though it was their first time sharing a bed together they both quickly fell asleep.

With everything appearing to be clear outside the fortifications Star decided that she was going to take Tempest for a short stroll outside the barricades. David was not keen on the idea trying to convince her to walk Tempest in the gated area behind the airport. She insisted that she would be perfectly fine with Tempest by her side. David knowing he could not change her mind went along with them saying he needed to stretch his legs anyway. A few blocks down David complained that they should head back to the airport. Starlette finally gave in after another block of listening to David moan that it wasn't safe. She called for tempest turning back around. A block and a half walking back, a bullet struck David in the stomach. He dropped to his knees holding his hands over the wound as blood seeped through his shirt.

About twenty feet away Starlette spotted the back of a large cargo truck sticking out beside what had been a small restaurant. A man ducked out of view before she could get a good look. The fur stood up on Tempest's back as she bared her fangs. She shot off in the direction of the restaurant. Starlette tried to call out for her to not go, but it came out in jumbled words.

The man appeared from the side of the building firing a shot at Tempest but missing. Knowing he had insufficient time to make another shot that counted he turned. Grabbing a latch at the back of the truck, he lifted the door up with a hard shove before bolting around the side for the safety of the truck's cab. Around fifteen *Fallen* poured out of the back of the truck. Tempest came to an abrupt halt slowly backing away while still ferociously baring her fangs. The *Fallen* came towards her not in the least frightened. She took off stopping a sufficient distance away before barking at them. She continued to do this slowly leading most away from the direction of David and Star. Only four stayed behind noticing easier pray or perhaps smelling the blood in the air. Starlette helped David to his feet the best she could while carrying half his weight. She headed for the nearest parked car as quickly as David's injury would allow. The *Fallen* that had noticed them were moving much faster than they could. One of them grabbed hold of Star right after she helped David inside the car. She fell to the ground trying to pull away. Noticing another was heading right for the open door, she used both feet to kick the car door shut.

Tempest had led the majority a good distance away before looking back in Starlette's direction. She saw that Star was in immediate danger. She took off running faster than she had ever ran in her life. Starlette was somehow keeping a second one at bay by using the one on top of her to block its advances. She kept both of her hands tightly around the first one's throat. Locking her elbows gave her small advantage. Even then, she began to lose the struggle as the horrid creature's strength was so overwhelming.

Drool fell on her face as gnashing teeth were mere inches away from her face. A sudden rush of adrenaline kicked giving Starlette an overwhelming strength of her own. She snapped its neck from the spine making it fall over to the side. Its teeth kept gnashing, but the rest of the body was unresponsive. The two that had been slower were now only a few feet away. The second one that was an immediate danger came at her now that there was nothing blocking its path. Tempest leapt through the air using her weight to knock it over. She tore out its throat at the same moment one of the slow *Fallen* pounced on her. It bit down on her leg ripping away a chunk of furry flesh. She yelped loudly which brought David around. He had been on the verge of blacking out, but the cry of pain snapped him fully awake. He spotted his gun that had fell in the floorboard when Star had helped him inside the car. He had been in such a hurry to follow Star that he completely forgot to put on the silencer. Quickly grabbing it up he shot the one that was attacking Tempest in the center of the head breaking the glass on the driver's side window in the process. The last one went straight for Starlette before David could turn to aim. It repetitively bit her in a rapid manner tearing flesh from her arms that she was using to protect her face. It hastily maneuvered enough using its strength to get past her arms sinking its rotten corroded teeth into her left cheek. Tempest turned her attention too late on the *Fallen* attacking Star, but she still knocked it away before mauling it. She then limped over laying down with Star while covered in blood that mostly belonged to the corpses of the Fallen. David saw that the larger group of *Fallen* were now heading in their direction about half a block away. Looking around he spotted the bookstore they had been to once before. The front door had previously been smashed in by Rye when they were hunting for books. He holstered his gun opening the driver's side door. He grimaced at the immediate pain pushing it out of his mind to do what needed to be done. He stepped out helping Star to her feet. They both helped each other walk as Tempest limped behind them. Tempest occasionally glanced back to see how close the *Fallen* were from them. At the front door Tempest barked since the Fallen were only ten feet away. Moving much quicker, David made his way towards the restroom that he knew had a locking door. Tempest did her best to distract the *Fallen*, even attacking one that had gotten ahead of the others. She heard Star call out to her. Tempest flew through the bookstore making her way to the restroom. David barely slammed the door closed locking it before the *Fallen* were pounding on it. He blacked out after dropping down to the ground.

The sound of a loud gunshot woke Dan from his short sleep. He shook April awake telling her there was trouble. They both jumped up grabbing assault rifles as they headed out the front of the airport. They saw several bodies lying on the ground near a car when taking a look through a pair of binoculars. Running at full speed, Dan grabbed April's arm pulling her to a stop a block away from the airport.

"That truck with the back open wasn't there before. I'm pretty sure I just saw someone moving around inside the cab."

Dan and April took cover behind bricked signage announcing the name of the airport. Dan aimed at the driver's window looking through the scope of the gun. A head popped up momentarily glancing in the side mirror before ducking back down.

"It's that psychopath that we left for dead. The preacher is still alive! How the hell did he get away from all those *Fallen*?"

"Seriously? Maybe he found some way to climb to the top of that building. Something else could have caught their attention I suppose. Doesn't really matter. I'm pretty sure David and Star are somewhere nearby in danger. We need to deal with the Preacher quickly so we can help them."

"On it."

Dan patiently waited for the Preacher to stick his head up again. The moment that he did Dan squeezed off the trigger. A little off target the bullet struck the preacher in the neck. Blood sprayed out the now broken window briefly. The Preacher grasped the wound tightly choking on his own blood. He slumped over onto the steering wheel making it go off. One of the *Fallen* from the bookstore came outside due to the noise. April pointed in its direction making sure Dan had noticed.

"That's probably where we will find them."

"Agreed. Switch your gun from single shot to automatic. We don't know how many we are dealing with. Be careful though. We don't want to hit the kids with stray bullets. We'll try to lead however many there are away from the building if possible before mowing them down with lead."

April followed Dan planning not to shoot until he gave the word unless in immediate danger. Dan walked in a direction to angle himself away from the bookstore. Meanwhile the *Fallen* out front noticed them. It began moving towards them with intestines hanging out of its chest that dragged on the ground. Ten feet away Dan took the kill shot before heading to the front of the building where it had come from. He yelled out making noise to attract any *Fallen* inside. April joined in banging on a nearby metal trashcan. Seeing a large group of *Fallen* suddenly appear coming from the back of the store they both moved to the left of the doorway stepping back about eight foot from there. They were now at an angle that they could shoot without bullets entering the store. The moment that the *Fallen* began exiting the building they started firing at them. There were so many bullets flying at close range that several of the *Fallen* were shredded like they were going through a cheese grader.  Limbs were hanging, large holes riddled their bodies that you could visibly see through, and yet they still kept coming. Dan began taking kill shots slightly pulling the trigger after aiming which resulted in two or three bullets per kill. There simply wasn't time to switch to singe shot. When it was all said and done there were eight *Fallen* piled up on the ground in front of the entrance. They were so torn up you could hardly tell they were once human.

"You think that's all of them?"

"Maybe. There could still be some of the intelligent ones that were smart enough not to wander out. If so they are likely lurking around where we will least expect them. Keep on guard, I go first. Just watch my back."

Inside they heard a noise off to the left. Dan turned in that direction while April glanced with her eyes, but kept focused on everything around them. A *Fallen* appeared from behind a few bookcases crouched down moving quickly over to the right.

"Behind you!"

She tried to get a good aim on it, but it took off back towards the way it had come after hearing her shout. Dan spun around not seeing any danger behind him.

"Their playing games. There has to be more than one. There is no way that one of them could have made it all the way around from that side to the other that quickly or without us noticing them down the center aisle. The one I saw took off as soon as I called out to you."

"Well, too bad for them there are also two of us. Plus they only retain parts of their intelligence. Let's see if we can outsmart them."

Moving as lightly as possible Dan began grabbing books and tossing them across the store in different directions. He listened each time one hit the floor for movement. At the same time they began making their way through the store sidestepping so that each was facing a different direction to be sure that they could not be snuck up on. At the drop of a fourth book, Dan heard a rustle behind a bookcase in the direction he had tossed it. He tapped April on the shoulder pointing for her to go to one side while he went to the other. They both made their way around the sides of the bookcase finding it empty. Dan immediately saw that one of the creatures was directly behind April. He raised his gun pointing in her direction. She understood exactly what was happening in a split second throwing herself to the ground. Dan took his shot as it began to run towards her. Several bullets knocked it down tearing large holes in its chest. Dan moved forward while continuing to fire. April rolled onto her back once Dan began shooting. She now took careful aim while still on her back before pulling the trigger when she was positive she had a perfect shot. Her bullet pierced the skull taking off a large portion of its forehead in the process. Dan quickly helped April up from the ground. Just as she was halfway up Dan saw another *Fallen* run out the front door.

"Looks like his partner just skedaddled out the front. We better still be precautious though in case there are any more. If the kids are in here they would have headed for the manager's office or the restrooms. Let's go see if we can find them."

Finding the manager's office empty they made their way to the restroom. The door was closed which gave them both hope that the kids were alright. Dan knocked on the door calling out to them. There was movement inside followed by the door being unlocked. As the door opened they saw Star standing in front of them with flesh torn from her face and arms. Blood was dripping on the ground. Her skin was as white as a ghost from the loss of blood."

April dropped to her knees covering her mouth from screaming. Tears welled up in her eyes.

"I'm so sorry, Star. I should have been quicker. I should..."

Starlette gently put a hand on Dan's lips stopping him from talking.

"I don't have much time. You're wasting your pity on the dead when you should be helping them."

Star fell down into a sitting position on the ground leaning back against a wall. Dan looked around noticing that David was covered in blood protruding from a hole in his shirt. Tempest had one of her legs amputated. Both of them were passed out.

"Tempest was bitten. I think the virus just kills animals. Didn't want to take a chance. David was shot in the stomach. You need to hurry if you're going to save them."

Seeing that both April and Dan were still somewhat distracted by her condition, Star reached over grabbing David's gun. She placed it below her jaw. Dan started to make a move to stop her.

"Help them now!" Starlette yelled before pulling the trigger. Her body toppled over falling halfway over Tempest.

April screamed becoming hysterical. Starlette's last words kicked Dan in the gut. He got to work immediately because they needed help, but also to honor Star's last wish. He talked in a firm voice trying to calm April while lifting Star's body. He laid her just outside the restroom before returning. Taking off his shirt he wrapped it around Tempest's leg. Then, he yanked off a shoestring tying it tightly around the shirt. Gently placing April's hands around the shirt, Dan told her to keep pressure on it. He pulled out a small pocket knife cleaning it off the best he could. Ripping open David's shirt he made a small incision just large enough to reach inside to pull out the bullet. Dan did what he could with the knowledge and supplies at hand. By then April had calmed down considerably.

"Wait here with them. Close the door just to be safe. I'm going to go get transportation so we can move them back to the airport."

April nodded her head. She locked the door after Dan pulled it closed. He jogged to the cargo truck that the Preacher had used yanking open the driver door without a thought. The reanimated *Fallen* corpse of the Preacher lunged at him. Dan instinctively sidestepped pushing the Preacher away from him. He glanced around for a weapon since he had mistakenly set his down in the restroom when attending to the injuries of the wounded. On the center console inside the vehicle was a hand-held hatchet in a sheath. He grabbed it before distancing himself a bit from the Preacher who had come close to biting him a moment before. Luckily, he had knocked the Fallen to the ground just in the nick of time with a right hook. He now pulled the hatchet from the sheath waiting for the Preacher to come at him again. When he did, Dan swung as hard as he could. The hatchet was so sharp that with the powerful swing it pierced right through the Preacher's skull like it were made out of butter. It made a loud cracking sound as fragments of bone broke being pushed into the brain along with the blade. He hopped in the cargo van driving over to the bookstore where he loaded the wounded in the back. Back at the airport he cleaned both of their wounds thoroughly with alcohol. Sterilizing and heating a flat scrap piece of metal a little bigger than the amputated area on Tempest's leg (which was still dripping blood even though tied off); Dan used it to cauterize the wound. April did her best to hold Tempest still during the process. She grimaced trying to pull away, but didn't attempt to bite like many dogs might have under similar conditions. Her heart was beating so fast it felt like it was going to come right out of her chest. April went off to find one of Starlette's old shirts for Tempest to snuggle up with while Dan proceeded to stitch up David's wound. He then wrapped clean sterile bandages around both of their injuries. Both of them were started on antibiotics along with extensive pain relievers. Plenty of pillows and blankets were piled up to make sure they were comfortable and warm. Dan walked off after he made sure they were fully cared for. April had to make a cone from a couple large plastic gallon water bottles to put around Tempest's neck because she kept trying to take off the bandage. After she finished that project she went to find out where Dan had wondered off to. She found him in the main lobby area staring out the large panel glass to the runway.

He was sitting in one of the many chairs smoking a cigarette.

"Since when did you start smoking?"

"Hmm, oh. I don't smoke. It's one of Kurt's. I just took a couple drags to calm my nerves. Just been letting it burn apparently since then. Lucky you came along. I probably would have burned my fingers since I was too preoccupied thinking instead of actually paying attention."

"What were you thinking about?"

"I was thinking about the fact that this would not have happened if I had ended the preacher that night."

"You can't put the blame for that on yourself. We all had the same opportunity. None of us thought there was a chance in hell he could have made it out of that situation or he would have been shot. We also needed the distraction he was making so that we could escape. Seriously, I know what just happened is horrible sweetheart, but it is not anyone's fault except for that psycho."

"I get what you're saying. I just wish that I had put a bullet in his head that night, then Star would still be alive. I also froze when I might have been able to help her like we did with Jessie. She had a chance even if it was a small one. I was in shock and terrified at the thought of losing all of them. Damn that girl for shooting herself, but if she hadn't those other two probably would be in their graves instead of fighting for their lives right now. I am to blame for all of that."

"Emotions get the best of all of us. We are all human. She wouldn't want you to feel like any of this was your fault. You know that! She would be thankful though for everything that you have done for Tempest and David."

April knelt down on her knees resting her head on Dan's arm. She stayed in that position for a while before getting up. She kissed Dan on the forehead telling him that she was heading off to the break room. About an hour later Dan came in to grab a warm beer and a can of peanuts. While chewing the peanuts he asked April what time it was. She told him that it was a little after two in the afternoon.

"About to go check on David if you want to come. Don't let me forget we need to be by the radio around five. I'm sure they will likely cut their trip short after we relay the bad news.

-2-

I woke up early as I often do. Leaving Rye and Amy to rest a couple more hours in the huge comfortable bed. I took another shower before changing into some warm clothes. In the kitchen I was able to use a coffee maker for the first time in years. It was much nicer than having to wait forever for the water to boil over an open flame. I then spent the next hour making a huge pile of pancakes for everyone. I had found a box of blueberry pancake mix that only required adding water. In the mix I tossed half a bag of Hersey's chocolate chips that was sitting in the cabinet next to it. The aroma from the coffee and pancakes woke the others up. They all trickled into the kitchen just as I finished cooking.

Amy had already set the table. Aurora had raided the cabinets finding four different kinds of pancake syrup. Kurt and Rye were sitting at the table enjoying their second cup of coffee. I gave everyone a stack of pancakes. When I placed food on Amy's plate she suddenly became extremely pale. She immediately ran off to the nearest bathroom. I went to check on her while the others ate their breakfast.

"You alright in there?"

The commode flushed prior to her opening the door.

"I think so. I feel a little better now. Not sure if I have a stomach bug or perhaps ate too much last night. The smell of the pancakes made me nauseous."

"Umm, sweetheart. You know, it could be something entirely different." Her eyes got big as the thought crossed her mind.

"You don't think? We've been using protection though."

"Not every time. There were a few times when the idea did not cross our minds in the heat of the moment. Also a couple when we were completely out of condoms. Even then protection doesn't always work."

"Oh god. If I am, how do you think Rye will take the news? For that matter, how do you feel about it? I'm not even sure how I feel."

"Calm down, hun. Take a deep breathe. First, we have to find out if you actually are. Second, both Rye and I would both be delighted."

"Yeah, but what if..."

"The epidemic? Surely the fact that we have probably built up some immunity has to count for something. There is no point over analyzing every aspect. You can't let yourself worry so much."

"Yes, but what about the *Fallen*? Do we really even want to bring a child into a world like this?"

"Alpine isn't so bad is it? If it doesn't work out here, we could build our own community. You know that

absolutely everyone in our group would protect our child.
Even Tempest would probably be watching over her most
hours of the day. He or she would always be safe in a
fortress guarded by those who loved them."

"K, I suppose you're right. We should try to find a
pregnancy test later today. If you don't mind helping me
look for one."

"If I don't mind? What planet are you on right now?
It will be just as much my child if you are pregnant. We
will get to looking right after breakfast."

Amy smiled as we headed back to the kitchen. She
was able to wolf down her pancakes with no further issues.
After breakfast I glanced out the window finding snow had
recently begun falling again. Across the street Peter was
standing in shorts and a t-shirt. He was holding a golf club
while looking down the block. I opened the front door
calling out to him.

"Are you seriously playing golf in the snow?"

He turned his head looking over in my direction
with a big goofy smile on his face.

"I'm one of those people that believe there is no
better time than the present to do things regardless of
circumstances. I was cleaning out a closet and found an old
golf bag. I've never tried it before so thought I would give

it a go. I'd probably play golf even if there were Fallen strolling around the streets. Of course, I would have a side-arm with me because I'm not completely mad."

"If I had a camera right now I would probably win some award for weirdest scene ever. That is of course providing the world had not changed. For that matter if I posted it on the internet I would probably be raking in the money on YouTube. I'd probably have a million hits just from one afternoon."

"Wouldn't be the first time I made headlines."

"I bet!" I walked across the street closing the door behind me. The others were peeking through the curtains as they were still in their pajamas. I could hear laughter coming from inside. Once across the street I spoke quietly to Peter. "I have a question for you."

"Okie dokie, what is it?"

"Where or who in town would I talk to about medications and feminine items?"

"Most of the medical supplies were moved to Dr. Chamberlain's clinic. She is the main doctor. We are fortunate to have a couple in our community."

"Where can we find the clinic or Dr. Chamberlain?"

I figure she should actually be by here around noon. She said that she was bringing a pumpkin pie by for one of your folks."

"Oh, so that was the doctor. I met her last night. The pumpkin pie would be for me. It is one of my favorite foods. Could eat it anytime of the year."

"I was always keen on chocolate mousse myself."

"So what are the plans for today?"

"After the doctor comes by I can show your group around town. You can all take in the amenities we have to offer. I'll also give you a gander at all the projects we have going on."

"Sounds good. Amy and I may not be able to attend the trip, unless of course we perhaps could find the doctor sooner. Really need to see her sooner if at all possible."

"She only lives a few blocks over. I can take you if it's that important. I'm sure she would be happy to give you a lift to the clinic if necessary."

"That would be great! I'll go tell Amy to get ready."

"Alright, no hurry. I'll be here perfecting my game when you're both ready."

I jogged across the street back to the guest house. Inside they were watching some anime on DVD.

"Amy, do you want to take a ride with me over to see the pumpkin pie lady?" Kurt made a snide remark about how I couldn't wait for more of that pie. "Turns out that woman is also the community's main doctor. Figured we could check out what kind of supplies they have. Maybe they can spare some for us to take back even if we decide not to move here."

Rye asked Amy if she was still not feeling well. He suggested that maybe the doctor could give her a once over. Amy said she was feeling considerably better. He then asked if we needed him to make the trip with us. I told him no, but Aurora was welcome to tag along with us if she wanted. That caught both the men's attention until I relayed that we were also going to ask about feminine products. That got both of them to quickly change subjects carrying on like they did not want to know in the least. Aurora was pleased to be invited to an outing with the girls.

"Looks like it is just you and me, Rye. We can veg with cold beer and play some football on the Xbox!"

"Ok boys don't miss us too much. No porn or parties while were gone."

"Ahh, you ruined our secret plans sis."

Aurora and Amy quickly got dressed. We kissed our men goodbye before heading out the door. Peter had already pulled his Lincoln Town Car out of the garage to warm it up. I tapped on the passenger window getting his attention. He motioned for us to hop inside. A few minutes later Peter was knocking on Dr. Chamberlain's door. She opened it up shaking her head at Peter.

"You know I have a doorbell. You realize that you look like a fool wearing shorts out in the snow, right? Were you trying to get sick as an excuse to pay me a visit?"

We all snickered at the doctor's direct way of speaking with Peter. Peter pretended he did not even hear the comment. He got straight to the point on why we were at her house. Introductions were made between everyone. Dr. Chamberlain told us to skip the formalities and simply call her Sarah. She told Peter that she would give us a lift back in a little while. She shooed him away with a hand gesture telling him to go put on some pants; preferably a jacket while he was at it.

Once inside she invited us to the kitchen where she was apparently waiting on the oven to warm up so she could put my pumpkin pie inside. We conversed a little mentioning that Amy had gotten sick this morning.

"So throwing up early in the morning? Was it a sudden nausea or had it been a lingering issue?"

"It was after I smelt the pancakes."

"Oh my, I'm guessing that you actually came for something other than nausea medication didn't you?"

"Actually, yes. We also thought perhaps we could check to see if you had any extra supplies to take back home with us in case of emergencies or common illnesses. At least that is the excuse we gave the men."

"The clinic isn't far. Should have more than enough time to swing by there before the pie is ready. Our supply of pharmaceuticals is limited. It's hard to keep a decent stock with such a large community. Plus, most are already expired so they are not as strong as they should be. We need to find a pharmacist and the supplies to make new medications to ideally continue to treat the population."

"My brother is actually a pharmacist. He likely knows what supplies would be necessary to make medications. Of course that depends on how hard the ingredients are to find or if they even still exist. He isn't exactly a chemist though. It would require someone who has experience actually making the medications providing the equipment necessary were available also."

"You are quite right. There might be a chemist here for all I know. Peter would have more information about that. We will have to ask him. However, it would be pointless unless your group actually move here."

"It is still under consideration. Doesn't mean that we couldn't work together somehow even if we decided not to move here," Aurora pointed out.

"Rightly so. I just wanted you to understand the predicament all of us are going to be facing eventually. I'm pretty sure I can whip together a small bag for you to take back with common medications."

"Thank you. We really appreciate everything you are doing for us," Amy said.

"Especially that pie!"

Sarah smiled at the fact that I enjoyed her pie so immensely. We headed to the clinic not long after the oven warmed up. She had us wait in the car with the heater running while she ran inside. She soon returned with a couple grocery bags full of medical supplies. She told Amy that the pregnancy tests were in one of them. Aurora had been filled in previously at Sarah's house. She was sworn to secrecy until we knew the results.

Sarah dropped us off back at the guest house. She promised to return soon with my pie before waving goodbye as she drove off. The guys were intensely playing video games with Peter who had been coerced to join.

Amy snuck off to the bathroom. Aurora and I huddled nearby in the hallway since the men were too preoccupied to even notice. A few minutes passed before she opened the door. Tears were streaming down her face, but she had a huge smile on her face. She held two different pregnancy tests which according to the boxes said that she was indeed pregnant. We both hugged her joining in with the tears of joy.

"Everything alright?" Rye had come around the corner to the hallway because he had heard the crying from the living room.

"Alright? Yes, everything is wonderful daddy," Amy told him.

"What?" His expression was shock for a couple seconds before it changed to complete excitement. "Seriously? So that was morning sickness with the pancakes? I can't believe I didn't even consider for a moment in my mind that was what caused you to get sick. This is great news though. I'm going to be a father!"

He grabbed both Amy and me giving us a huge hug while lifting us partially off the ground. Then he ran off to the living room to share the good news. As we walked in the living room there were congratulations from both Kurt and Peter, who looked about as excited as Rye had been on initially finding out. Kurt was delighted that he was going to be an uncle.

"I suppose we are going to have to work on a nursery as a welcome gift. That is of course if you choose to move to Alpine."

"The prospect is looking like a good idea. Let's go check out the rest of town like you suggested this morning. I'm sure we will have a definite answer soon."

"As soon as we finish this one game. You are still waiting on a pie right?"

"My pie! I completely forgot about it."

Sarah showed up around noon, right when Peter had predicted she would. I ate it for lunch while the others had Frito Pie without cheese. Peter told us that they had two dairy cows, but the process to turn it into cheese was complicated. Apparently most of the community would rather have the milk anyway because it was in short supply to begin with. Sarah didn't stay for long as she had some patients to check in on.

-3-

After lunch, Peter began showing us the various important locations around Alpine. We visited the power plant first. The electricity had been modified to use solar and wind energy collectors to supply energy to the main power grid on top of its existing main power source. There was supposedly a three man crew that knew how to work on everything at the facility. The water reformation site was running smoothly without issues. He said that they originally had a problem with the water infecting a few citizens. The entire system had to be enclosed so that it did not collect the water from the rain or snow directly. The purification of those forms of water as they were absorbed through the earth worked where other forms of cleaning the water previously had not. Other than the underground water aquifers were the main supply of water, but they also obtained water from various other sources that were processed through the main purification system to be reused.

The gas company was the major concern Peter had. They were quickly running out of a viable source of fuel. They tried to use it as sparingly as possible, but after two hard winters it was almost depleted. On top of that all of the gas was bad by now. Fuel stabilizers even with the best gas normally only stayed fresh for about a year and a half tops. Before long we would all be walking. Peter told us that they had acquired a couple of solely solar powered and electric powered vehicles for when it did come to that. However, everyone would be without heat or hot water any day now. He then mentioned that two new men that recently joined the community knew a few things about refining oil and the whole process to make new gas. Peter told us that they previously worked on oil drilling rigs among other things. Whatever they didn't know could be learned from books or manuals according to what they told him. The complicated part would be finding volunteers to help with the work, however long it took to teach them, and securing the facilities for the entire process.

"If your community went without gas for a winter I'm sure there would be a long line of volunteers. Trying to stay warm around a campfire or huddled under a dozen blankets will make anyone jump to helping out."

"Hopefully, it won't come to such drastic measures. Still plenty to see."

Peter drove us to a large area used for crops, the hunting grounds, and finally the business district. Peter was delighted to inform us that citizens had volunteered to provide different services and products as a way to provide to the community as a whole. It was up to the individual whether they wanted to trade or swap services. Some in the community even provided services for free to those that were in need. However, if there were major disagreements of fair trade among the people, they were reported. If there were constant reports from various sources about the same person then the one causing the problems could be suspended from trade or services, as well as fined. It had not happened as of yet, but on the third violation instead of suspension they would be permanently banned from setting up in the business district.

Walking around we saw that there was a citizen ran bakery, small newspaper group (daily articles written on a single sheet of paper), a coffee shop, a vet clinic, and several other businesses.

Peter told us that there were other positions that the citizens were employed at such as at the post office (basically a runner that took ran messages for other people), a small fire brigade, a trash collector, and three people that handled law enforcement.

I asked him the specifics of exactly how the law system worked. I was curious what kind of crime they had to deal with on a daily basis. I also wondered if they had some kind of court proceedings to decide sentencing. Peter told us that crime was very minimal. An occasional public intoxication or fist fight were the biggest issues. Those individuals usually got locked up for a day followed by consultation with a counselor. There had been a couple repeat offenders. In those instances they were locked up for three days followed by being informed that if they repeated the crime they would be banned from Alpine. They would then have to see a specialist for a week to discuss their problems on ways to work around them. If it was a drinking problem then they would be sent to get help with old members of an AA group. They would also have someone shadow them for a month to help them stay clean. Only one person has ever not taken the warning to heart repeating a crime for a third instance. His name was Gabriel Mendoza. He was taken to the city of Marfa where he was dropped off. As much as he pleaded that he would not repeat his mistakes, the process had to be followed through as an example for the others. He was left with supplies being told not to return to Alpine for at least a year. If at that time he wished to return, then he would have to have a formal meeting with the Committee of Five. This committee Peter explained was a group of elders directly under him that dealt with various important issues such as new directions the community as a whole should take. They were basically a think tank with other minor responsibilities. At the same time if they did not agree with a choice that Peter made they could override his decision with a three of five vote to do so.

While having a cup of coffee, we passed around one of the daily newspaper articles. Peter told us that they always gave the first one away for free to get you hooked. A woman came up to the table while we were sitting around relaxing. She looked very familiar. It took me a moment to realize who it was without the chauffeur outfit and hat.

"Been a while since I saw you and Kurt. This must be other members of your group?"

"Celeste, it's nice to see you. I didn't notice you at last night's festivities," I said.

"Hello to you too daughter."

"Sorry dad, was just excited to see them." She turned back to look in my direction after apologizing to her father. "Unfortunately, I was out of town. I was out on a supply run with a couple others in Pecos for a few days. We made it in around three in the morning."

"Glad you made it back safely munchkin."

"Dad! You know I hate it when you call me that. I'm twenty-four now, not three."

"Sorry pumpkin. Have any luck? Run into any problems?"

"Nothing we couldn't handle. We actually found a large nest of supplies. Ran across two survivors too. They are considering coming to visit sometime after winter.

Pretty sure they didn't believe half the stuff we told them of course."

"Maybe we should make the details of the community sound more believable. Tell them less perhaps. Surprise them with the whole grand tour when they show up."

"I still don't believe it even though I've seen it," Rye said.

We all laughed feeling about the same way Rye described it. Everyone introduced themselves. Celeste joined us for coffee and conversation for a while. A little after four in the afternoon, Rye reminded Peter that we needed to radio the group back home. Peter told us there was a military radio at the nearby sheriff's office we could use.

At five o'clock Rye was just getting in contact with the others back home. The rest of us were conversing with Curtis Wright in his office. He was the head of the law enforcement group for Alpine. He wore a sheriff's badge from San Angelo pinned to his uniform. Apparently, all three of the current law enforcement officers had previous experience in this type of field. A few minutes into our conversation a woman wearing an Oklahoma City Police Department uniform came into the office. After getting our

185

attention she let us know that there had been trouble at the airport. She didn't have much of the details, but relayed that Rye was asking for us. We all followed her to the communications room. On entering the room all we heard were the last two sentences Rye said over the radio.

"We're on our way. We'll try to get there as soon as possible."

Rye spun the chair he had been sitting in around, quickly standing up.

"We have to go back immediately. The Preacher somehow survived. He attacked them. All hell has broken loose!"

There was a long pause of silence as we tried to grasp how he could have survived. We all became extremely worried still unclear of what had happened.

"Calm down love. Tell us what happened." I tried staying calm while attempting to find out the specifics of what occurred.

"He brought a truck full of *Fallen*, waited for the right opportunity, and created havoc is what happened. David got shot. Both Star and Tempest were bitten."

Everyone suddenly became emotional trying to talk over each other. They were all beginning to panic which wasn't helping anyone.

"Everyone calm down please." I had to almost yell to be heard. "Rye, what is the current condition of everyone? What can we do to help?"

"Dan took out the Preacher permanently this time. Apparently the kids were on guard duty while the adults were getting some sleep. Not clear why they left the airport, but somehow they ended up at the nearby bookstore. The Preacher must have shot David in the stomach at some point which woke Dan from his sleep. They had to deal with a large group of Fallen to get to the kids. Star and Tempest had already been attacked by Fallen before the three of them secured themselves in the bookstore's restroom. Dan found that Star had amputated Tempest's leg hopefully saving her life. They are under the impression that the virus outright kills animals if infected. Dan pulled out the bullet that pierced David's stomach before stitching him up. Star..." He had to stop for a minute choking up on finding the right words. "Starlette sacrificed herself to save the other two. She had been bitten multiple times. In the end she took her own life with David's gun so that the adults would focus on helping them instead of stare in shock at her condition."

Ryes words were followed by confusion, tears, and condolences to us from the members of Alpine in the room.

Thirty minutes later we were packing up the RV. Peter insisted on sending a few people out this afternoon to provide assistance. We agreed giving him our exact location. He promised to send one of their doctors and a vet who had years of experience dealing with animals. We thanked him before getting on our way back to Salt Flat.

We made it back in under four hours even with the bad road conditions. It was heartbreaking seeing David and Tempest in their current states. The loss of Starlette was like being hit by a semi-truck. It had to have been horrible for David to lose the girl he had grown so close to and fallen in love with. Dan was taking things pretty hard. He had been the one to collect Star's body which was currently covered in a sheet in one of the hanger bays.

Around midnight a small procession of cars arrived with their headlights shining brightly on the snow. They stopped short of the blockades identifying themselves as individuals from Alpine. There were twelve men and women in all. Dr. Chamberlain, Curtis, and other faces we recognized. The vet Peter promised was also among the group. They brought lots of supplies including food.

It was an extremely long night with all the company showing up so late. We made accommodations for their party when several decided they needed to get some rest.

Sarah stayed up fussing over David. The vet which went by the name of Todd kept a close watch on Tempest. Their wounds were redressed after checking for any signs of infection. They were both given sedatives and pain killers so they could sleep as much as possible. Dan was congratulated on doing exemplary work with both of them under the circumstances.

In the morning, Peter told us that those providing medical care would stay behind for as long as they were needed. He said if there was absolutely anything we required not to hesitate getting in touch with him. He also reminded us that Alpine was an open invitation if we chose to move.

We had a small funeral for Starlette during the afternoon a few days later. David pulled through attending in a wheel chair. He was not just physically in bad shape. He had not said a single word since finding out that Star did not make it. When we tried to make direct conversation he simply stared off in the distance or seemingly right through you. I had seen the same look before on soldiers faces after going through hell or losing close comrades whilst being there when it occurred.

I still recall the first time I saw someone with PTSD back at the Marines training camp. There was a kid named

Bobby who was fresh out of high school. Wanting to do something important with his life, he had enlisted. He was top of the class in everything we did. I'll admit that I was envious always coming in second, but I would not wish what happened to him on anyone.

One of the other guys we had nicknamed KitKat because of his infatuation with the candy he was unable to have during training became Bobby's closest friend. One day during training exercises a live grenade went off in the field. Both Bobby and KitKat were in the area when it happened. Apparently KitKat threw himself on top of it out of instinct not knowing it was live or even thinking for a moment that it was not. Bobby had to witness his closest friend die before his very own eyes.

No matter how hard the psychologists attempted to get through to Bobby, he remained in a state of shock and horror staring off into space without a word. He would occasionally scream at some unseen horror that he relived every day. He was eventually sent home after they graduated him with honors. It was their hope that he would eventually recover with some time off away from where the accident occurred. He never did return or have a normal life after that. He had moments of cognition, but usually remained in a state of post-traumatic stress. I heard that about seven years after being sent home from the Marines that he had been involved in a massive shootout in a small city mall near his home. He had killed four people, injured another eighteen, and then turned the gun on himself ending his life.

# Chapter 6
# End of the Road

-1-

Peter and the others left after the funeral with the exception of Sarah and Todd. I had a short conversation about David with Peter prior to them leaving. He promised to have Celeste return with a prominent psychologist in hopes it could help David more than the ones that had helped Bobby.

Celeste returned a week later. The psychologist after spending an hour with David told us that he was pretty far gone. She had only been able to get a word or two out of him at most. Her suggestion was to take David to Alpine as an environmental change. She also thought he needed around the clock observation. We agreed that it was probably for the best.

After much consideration we let Celeste know that we would be moving to Alpine. We told her it would take a week or two before we headed that way. She said that she would relay the message having the guest house prepared until we found suitable residences that we liked. Tempest was already hobbling around begging for attention. I suggested that she go with David to keep him company. The psychologist readily agreed that it was a great idea. She thought it might be helpful for his therapy. They all left out that evening taking David and Tempest with them.

Overnight the snow fell extremely heavy. By morning it was blizzard conditions outside. The atmosphere seemed to be purging itself completely of any last abnormalities it might have had. I had not seen a blizzard this bad in almost twenty years. Not that it was a concern for us, but I recalled the major power outages among other things of that past storm. During my recollection I thought about Alpine. I could only imagine that they were likely now in the same conditions as us trying to make do without power. I figured they were probably trying their damnedest to stay warm. Hopefully, it had not affected them as devastatingly as I imagined. However, the odds were not in their favor.

Packing to leave was out of the question. We became too preoccupied huddling together around a fireplace at a house near the airport which we had secured months ago in case it was necessary due to such weather. It also made good for a hasty escape from the airport if we ever needed it. There was a large pile of wood we had gathered after securing the house which constantly fed the fire. We huddled the best we could to stave off the cold.

We had prepared for a worst case scenario beforehand which likely is the only reason we survived the rest of November in that house. The blizzard became a light snow at the beginning of December. Unfortunately, the currently waist high snow made it impossible to travel farther than a short distance outside of which we worked to keep clear so we would not become trapped inside.

Another week passed before the sun protruded enough to begin melting some of the snow during the daylight hours. A few days of the sun created flooding. It was difficult to keep the water out of the house. At night the water would freeze over leaving sheets of ice to maneuver carefully around outside.

Mid-December we made our way back to the airport. If not for the heater in the truck we would have been frozen human popsicles on arrival. Packing or anything else was a major hassle with body parts going quickly numb. After a few hours we retreated back to the truck to warm ourselves. We made a couple more trips before being too physically exhausted to continue any further. We locked up the vehicles with our belongings before heading back to the house with the fireplace.

At the very slow pace we were going plus days off to recuperate it would be January before we could make the trip providing the weather allowed us to. The seven of us had five vehicles in all to drive. It was decided April would ride with Dan, Amy with Rye, while the rest drove individually. Christmas was temporarily postponed. On the third of January we finally headed out. The trip was slow going because of the ice. The sun had not come out today. Instead a gray sky produced light rain to hinder our progress further.

This part pains me to write beyond description. There are no words to truly express how I feel, but I will do my best to simply put down what happened. During our commute we attempted to stay close to the vehicles in front of us. Dan was at the head of the procession and Rye was at the tail end.

A deer came out of the woods on the right in front of Dan. We all lightly hit our brakes in unison slowing down. As everyone sped back up, a *Fallen* ran out further down heading the direction the deer had gone. Aurora who was in front of me passed in front of it before it made it to the road. I swerved not to hit it, afraid it might come flying right through the windshield. Rye who was behind me had to hit his brakes hard because my truck started sliding on the ice. Every time I tried to correct the vehicle the ice made it over-correct sliding the opposite direction so that I was fishtailing. When Rye had hit his breaks, the truck slid hard to the left flipping. It rolled twice before coming to a complete stop. I held down the horn to get the others attentions as I finally got my vehicle under control slowing to a crawl.

On inspection the two of them were disoriented, but perfectly fine. The *Fallen* which had ran in front of me was pinned under their truck flailing about. We helped them out of the truck. Dan gave them a once over while I finished off the *Fallen* for good measure.

After making sure they were ok, Rye and Amy sat on a broken tree log just off the side of the road. The rest of us rifled through the stuff packed in the rolled truck. We moved anything important to the other vehicles stuffing what we could into wherever it would fit.

As they sat on the log trying to recuperate their senses, two *Fallen* ran out of the woods behind them. Rye heard one of them break a branch on the ground barely before they reached them. He pulled Amy up shouting at her to run. He then drew his side arm shooting one in the head. At the same time the other leapt in his direction knocking him to the ground. He lost his gun in the process.

They rolled around with Rye doing his best to keep the *Fallen* from biting him. We all dropped what we were doing to face whatever threat we were facing when we heard Rye yell at Amy to run. The *Fallen* attacking Rye was one of the intelligent ones. It saw that we were drawing our guns; immediately going crazy clawing and biting Rye several times before Aurora got a shot off. It fell over onto its side with blood pouring out of its neck, but was still moving. Rye rolled grabbing his gun on the ground finishing it off.

We ran to Rye who was in bad shape. The snow was covered in blood. Aurora tried to stop me from getting near Rye, but I easily maneuvered around her. He had scratches and bites on his arms. Part of his right ear was missing. There were deep scratches on his face. Worst of all, Rye's shirt was torn open. The flesh had been ripped open exposing his rib cage. One of the ribs had been snapped so that it was puncturing a lung and protruding upward out of the cavity. He was coughing up blood on top of that.

"Oh Rye, not like this! We can't lose you now." I was on my knees in front of him with tears pouring down my face holding one of his hands.

"Help me sit up." He struggled getting the words out coughing up more blood.

Dan and Kurt lifted him gently sitting him with his back against the log they had previously been sitting on. Amy and I were both crying trying to lightly hug him with our heads rested on his shoulders. The others kept their guard up for more *Fallen* trying to block out their emotions the best they could even though they too were silently shedding tears.

"I love you...both. Take care of...each other. I'll always be watching over you." He rested a hand on Amy's belly. "And this one."

We broke down shaking while we were crying so intensely. He did his best to hug us both tightly. He kissed each of us on the forehead.

"You need to go...before I turn. There's not much life left...in me. Go! Now!" He shouted the last two words pushing us away while coughing really badly.

We tried to argue and stay near him as emotionally distraught as we were. The others had to pull us away. Aurora and April did their best to comfort us while leading us to the vehicles. Dan and Kurt stayed behind. Rye looked over at Kurt.

"Keep them safe. Protect them." He then looked at Dan who was tearing up. "We've been through a lot old friend. Lead them...the best you can. Do whatever you feel...is right for our family. No matter how hard...the choice or action do what is necessary for their surv..." Rye reached out grasping Dan's arm in a final embrace. He closed his eyes as his head slumped onto his chest. Both Dan and Kurt backed away.

Dan lifted his revolver pointing it precisely. He pulled the trigger making sure Rye did not turn, leaving him in all our memories as the man we knew instead of some creature.

Leaving the rest of the remaining things in the overturned truck we left immediately. Amy rode with April in one vehicle. Dan took over driving the one I had been driving while I rode with Aurora. They knew that both of us were more emotionally compromised than the rest to be driving. We didn't go over fifteen miles an hour for the rest of the way to Alpine. The loss of Rye hit everyone harder than anyone we had lost over the last couple years. Peter and the rest of the community tried their hardest to accommodate our every need. Celeste was sent out with a small party to retrieve Rye's body. We had a burial funeral for him a few days after arriving in Alpine. Everyone gave their condolences while letting us privately mourn our loss. We stayed in a funk for a week following the funeral. Peter had a brainstorm on getting us out of the rut we were in.

Peter put together a play using several members of the community including children. It was a hilarious skit. As hard as we tried not to laugh we all eventually did before it was over. Laughter is as they say, good for the soul. The only person that did not crack a smile was David who was lost in another world of his own thoughts paying no attention at all to the play.

I'm not saying the play fixed all our problems or made us forget our losses. It was a start to a long path of healing. After the play there was a social gathering. There were a few that had late Christmas presents for us. The rest had given us presents throughout the week. During that week our states of mind perceived them pretty much meaningless holding no comfort from the pain. I even let a pumpkin pie go uneaten until it had to be thrown out. Now we felt a little guilty for not appreciating everything that the people of Alpine had done for us. The one person that really brought that feeling to the forefront for me was the little girl Stephanie. She ran up to me with her arms open wanting a hug. I bent down to give her the affection she was seeking. Hugging her made me cry. She patted me on the back telling me it was going to be alright. Afterwards, the man who was now her father figure walked up handing her a small wrapped present that she gave to me.

"Stephanie insisted on bringing this for you. She wrapped it herself. Not sure what it even is to be honest."

I reached out taking it from her small hands. Before opening it I thanked her for the present telling her it was very sweet of her. Inside the wrapping I found a stuffed white teddy bear. I gave Stephanie another hug before she ran off to play with some of the other kids.

"I'm really surprised she gave you her bear."

"Why is that?"

"It was the only possession she had when I found her. She had been surviving off of candy bars and juice boxes inside a van parked in front of a roadside gas station. Apparently her mother had gone inside, but never came back out. The bear has been her security blanket forever. It was something to remember her parents by I suppose."

"That's horrible. I can't take her bear."

"You have to. It will hurt her feelings if you don't. She wanted you to have it. Plus maybe it is her way of finally letting go. She will always have her memories of them, but now she can move forward without the weight of the past."

I nodded my head before walking outside where I broke down in tears. His words and the realization of Rye being gone hit me hard again. Amy was soon by my side having overhead everything that occurred with Stephanie and her caretaker. She took my hands placing them gently on her stomach.

"Rye will continue on through this one, through us, through our friends, and loved ones. He gave his life to protect those he loved. There is no greater sacrifice or thing to be remembered for. He was a wonderful man who loved and cherished every moment he spent with us or others. He was a natural leader that always provided for everyone doing his best to keep us safe every single day. He slayed monsters in a world gone to shit. He was many, many things and he will be remembered for them all in our hearts and our memories."

I had listened to every word she said while teary eyed. When she finished I threw my arms around her. We both wept in each other's arms for a long period of time. Without her there to comfort me or give me words of encouragement I would likely give up seeing no future in this world.

A month passed quickly as time often does. We had found houses that were to our liking. Seeing how none of us wanted to be separated we all took up residence in the same neighborhood. To be more specific our houses were all next door to one another. Dan and April thought it was best if David not be left stuck in some clinic when they could just as easily take care of him. They took him and Tempest in at their place. Somehow Tempest kept escaping their back yard only to be found on our front porch. She would be there wagging her tail in the mornings the moment she saw Amy. They finally gave up trying to take her back to their house for David's sake.

One night as everyone was preparing to settle in for sleep, Tempest started howling really loud. The next moment we heard a gunshot. I immediately knew what had happened without a second guess. We exited the house finding Tempest laying with her head on her paws looking forlorn. The lights were on over at Dan's place. Kurt and Aurora came out of their house a few seconds later.

As I guessed David had managed to get hold of a gun taking the worst way out of life and suffering. April was very shaken up. The mess was so bad that we had to cut the carpet up and scrub the walls for hours. Dan again tried taking all the blame believing he should have hidden the guns better. I told him that it would not have mattered. If David did not find a gun he would have found another way. My logic eventually got through to him enough so he would stop blaming himself.

The following day we contacted Peter letting him know what had happened. There was a big funeral with at least half the population showing up. He was buried near Rye at Slumberhaven cemetery. Peter made a speech for David explaining the illness from which he had suffered to those attending who did not understand why a young man had taken his life.

Later that day I recorded more details in the journal that Rye had left behind. Some days I like to write for several hours. Others I look back reading the words he left behind. This journal has become what the teddy bear was to Stephanie, my security blanket and my solace. Perhaps someday I will pass it on as she did with the bear to finally let go of the past. Maybe I will give it to the little one Amy carries in her womb, so they will have something to know their parents by. All three of us!

-2-

A few days later Peter let us know that tombstones had been erected on both graves at Slumberhaven. In March we went to visit them finding fresh flowers adorning both. The rain fell later that day once again without any hint of impurifications. It was freezing cold, but it felt wonderful. In the rain Amy and I kissed for the first time since Rye had passed away. It wasn't because we didn't love one another or were having problems of any kind. It was simply that the thought of kissing made us both think of Rye up until then. This time it was different somehow. We looked into each other's eyes and only the two of us existed in that moment. The kiss was passionate rekindling the romance that we had previously avoided. We decided to have a small private wedding during that month followed by a nice honeymoon at a recently secured cabin in the woods.

Recording that moment in the journal has got me thinking. I'm sure there are things in both Rye's and my own words that you could do without the details of. Plus it may not be age appropriate. You will likely have to reach a certain age before I even consider handing this journal over. I apologize if anything we have written grossed you out, made you sad, frightened you, or anything else. That was never our intentions.

In April Amy began having labor pains. It happened during the day while we were walking through the business district. We had plenty of assistance making it to St. Michaels Minor Emergency Clinic which was the closest. It was bigger than Sarah's clinic being ran by Dr. Davis and a small staff of three others. Regardless of his credentials or experience Amy demanded that Sarah was going to be the one to deliver the baby. She was quickly located and brought to the clinic.

Amy's water broke within an hour of Sarah's arrival. The most beautiful baby girl was born soon after. You had the same blue eyes and dark brown hair as your father which made everyone smile.

The men went outside to celebrate with cigars while your mothers and aunts took turns holding you. Yes, I say your aunts because not long after you were born there was a huge double wedding, but we'll get to that in a moment.

Amy and you were kept at the clinic for three days for observation to make sure there were no complications. You were the first one born that anyone knew of since the epidemic first began. It was a comforting thought for everyone being that the explosion occurred exactly three years ago this month. You gave everyone hope that life would continue and the human race would thrive again making a better place out of a darkened world. You were not only our light at the end of the tunnel. You were the spark that gave everyone hope which is why we named you Ember.

Peter was true to his word. As we got home we found a nursery completely decked out with everything you could possibly need. There was so much pink it was almost sickening. As overwhelming as it is you will likely come to despise the color as you grow older.

In July, Aurora and April were both proposed to by Amy's brothers. Huge preparations were made by the entire population of Alpine for a massive wedding to occur the following month. They both had the most beautiful wedding dresses, expensive rings, and colorful bouquets. There were limousines, a huge cake, and flowers everywhere. The feast was bigger than I can recall at any wedding I have ever attended.

Amy and I were both ecstatic that the others were deservingly happy after all this time. I suppose this is a good place as any to end my journal and set aside that metaphorical teddy bear I no longer need. I have Amy and you. You're my teddy bear now. You will both guide and comfort me in the days to come.

## -Epilogue-

It has been a couple years since I wrote in this thing. I just happened to come across it while cleaning. You're now two years old growing like a sprout. You look even more like your father. You're running around getting into everything you possibly can.

You're uncle Kurt is helping to work on the oil refinery project. Uncle Dan is working with a chemist on a new pharmaceutical project. Aunt Aurora works with Celeste. She goes out of the city to find supplies for the population. Aunt April is working at a bakery. She makes quite a delicious pumpkin pie if I do say so. Amy your biological mother stays home full-time taking care of the little rascal that you are. Lastly, there is me (your other mother, who will always protect and love you like my own). When I'm not home helping to take care of you, I'm out working security and defense detail. I make sure that this town is always safe from *Fallen* that dwell outside the walls.

We are all extremely careful. Most of the community barely ever go outside the fences where the danger lies. For those like your Aunt Aurora who do so because it is necessary, we all have our parts to play so those here continue to stay safe, fed, and to have the medical supplies they need among other things.

That reminds me, the whole purpose of adding to the journal was I wanted to say a few things. Some of what I have to tell you may sound bleak, but bear with me until the end. There is no promise on life. That is why you must stay safe. Prepare for the worst no matter what you do or where you go.

No future is guaranteed. The *Fallen* could overrun us tomorrow. There could be other large communities that might join us in our endeavors or attempt to attack us. The *Fallen* might simply cease to exist whether by conditions of the environment, by another horrible weapon the former President finds at his disposal, or something else. What I am trying to say is things happen. Some of them will be out of your control to change. However, you will always have the choice to make your own path and carve your own future. Always consider your options. Knowledge is more powerful than the strength of a hundred *Fallen*. Know your enemy, know their weaknesses, learn to defend yourself, and always protect those who cannot protect themselves.

Hope and love are the greatest powers on Earth. They can overcome anything and everything. They will lead you in your darkest days. Keep hope and love alive inside you. Never let them go. Even if your time comes to an end, those two things will live on in others if you fill their hearts.

There is solace and light in the world. For me you are those things. I am not alone in that perception. For others it might be smaller things. Find that which gives you peace of mind in difficult times. Find your own light that gives you the strength to overcome all obstacles.

I know that you have a great purpose. Never be a follower. Make your own way. You have no need to prove yourself to others, only yourself. Don't 'try' to lead, trying and doing are two different things. A true leader leads by example. They do everything for others, never themselves. Take advice from others, but make decisions that you know are the right ones. If that option is not available then choose the one that keeps you aligned closest to your morals or goals. Occasionally, you may give in on little things, but never the big choices that matter the most. Stand firm and don't back down from anyone on those occasions. Learn to let others help you. You cannot change the world by yourself.

The last thing I want to say is we love you. I love you Ember. May your path be one that leads to a brighter world.

**-End of Book 2-**

Another book in the trilogy completed! Hope you enjoyed reading it as much as I did creating the story. Thank you to my returning and new readers to my work. For those of you that may be upset at a favorite character dying, please understand this is an apocalyptic world...anything can happen. It is not my intention to kill of cherished individuals any more than you enjoy reading about their deaths. The story has a life of its own. Changing the structure of what transpires to suffice my own desire for them to live would make for a story that no one would want to read (because I would rather let them all live). Every death has a purpose and the sacrifices they make for others show that humanity and love live on even in a dark world.

Author Pages:
Twitter
https://twitter.com/MartinWFrancis
Facebook
https://www.facebook.com/MartinWFrancis
Instagram
Darkangel13777
Email Author
Darkangel13777@hotmail.com
Publisher
http://www.facebook.com/darkstormpress

To send mail for author:
Dark Storm Press
C/O Martin W. Francis
2515 62nd St
Lubbock, TX 79413

www.ingramcontent.com/pod-product-compliance
Lightning Source LLC
Chambersburg PA
CBHW070832120626
46556CB00002B/733

* 9 7 8 0 6 9 2 5 3 7 7 1 8 *